Fiona Robertson is a writer and doctor. Her short fiction has been published in literary magazines and anthologies in Australia and the UK, and has been shortlisted for international competitions. Her collection of stories, *If You're Happy*, won the Glendower Award for an Emerging Queensland Writer at the 2020 Queensland Literary Awards. Fiona lives in Brisbane with her husband and children.

Book club notes are available at www.uqp.com.au

IF YOU'RE HAPPY

FIONA ROBERTSON

First published 2022 by University of Queensland Press
PO Box 6042, St Lucia, Queensland 4067 Australia

University of Queensland Press (UQP) acknowledges the Traditional Owners and their
custodianship of the lands on which UQP operates. We pay our respects to their Ancestors
and their descendants, who continue cultural and spiritual connections to Country.
We recognise their valuable contributions to Australian and global society.

uqp.com.au
reception@uqp.com.au

Cover design by Josh Durham, Design by Committee
Author photograph by Sheona Beach
Typeset in 12/17 pt Bembo Std by Post Pre-press Group, Brisbane
Printed in Australia by McPherson's Printing Group

This manuscript won the 2020 Glendower Award for an Emerging Queensland Writer, which
is generously supported by Jenny Summerson. UQP launched the Emerging Queensland
Writer Award in 1999. Presented as part of the Queensland Literary Awards, in partnership with
State Library of Queensland, UQP is proud to publish the annual award-winning manuscript,
and is committed to building the profile of, and access to, emerging writers in Australia and
internationally.

This project has been assisted by the Australian
Government through the Australia Council, its arts
funding and advisory body.

A catalogue record for this book is available from the National Library of Australia.

ISBN 978 0 7022 6346 0 (pbk)
ISBN 978 0 7022 6540 2 (epdf)
ISBN 978 0 7022 6541 9 (epub)
ISBN 978 0 7022 6642 3 (kindle)

University of Queensland Press uses papers that are natural, renewable and recyclable products
made from wood grown in well-managed forests and other controlled sources. The logging and
manufacturing processes conform to the environmental regulations of the country of origin.

For Dad (Bruce) and Mum (Leonie).
This book began with you.

CONTENTS

TEMPEST

THEY ARE HAVING SEX WHEN the wind starts up, whispering and sighing outside. Shelley listens, her hands on Jay's shoulders, but her husband just pulls her closer and starts muttering in her ear, a running commentary of what he's doing and how good he'll make her feel. Jay has done the talking thing for years – since their first sneaky sex in his parents' barn. The time to tell Jay she doesn't like the talking has come and gone; it's part of their routine, like the way she brews their coffee with four big scoops, or how Jay hangs his hat on her Zulu statue, ignoring the hat rack beside it.

The bedroom is dark. It's just after six, the sun not yet risen. The only glow is the alarm clock as they move in the way they've always moved. Jay smells of soap from last night's shower. Shelley runs a hand down his broad, fleshy back, softness over muscle, and tries to block out his hot murmurs and the sound beyond their room. If she can shut her eyes and absorb the sensations, her body will respond.

A howl curls around the farmhouse and she pulls away. 'Jay. There's a storm out there.' It is early May, Texas thunderstorm season. She is alert and hopeful.

'It's fine, Shell. Just the wind.' Jay's eyes are half-closed.

She knows she won't get common sense from him, not now. She wriggles off the bed, pulling on her bathrobe. 'I'll check the weather site. There might be a warnin'.'

She flicks the hall light on and pads away, tying the belt from habit, though the children have grown and gone. She passes the bedrooms either side – one a dusty guest room and the other full of boxes, an old pedestal fan and the ironing board. A knot twists in her stomach and she strides to the kitchen.

~

Shelley is leaning over the laptop when Jay appears in the dim light of dawn. He's wearing sweatpants and a T-shirt, and the skin is puffy beneath his eyes. Yesterday was a long day, spraying the herd for horn fly.

He peers at the screen. 'Anythin'?'

Shelley shakes her head. 'Just a thunderstorm watch.'

Lightning flashes over cupboards and walls before the kitchen returns to shadows. For a moment there is silence, then thunder rumbles in the distance.

'Well, sure. I coulda told them that.' Jay touches her wrist. Shelley knows what he hopes but she's not going back to bed. She's waiting for the storm.

When a storm approaches, she tingles and breathes and comes alive. She forgets how Jay drives her crazy with his plodding ways, wanting steak or fried chicken day after day, forgets how his idea of travel is eating at a diner in Muleshoe instead of Dimmitt. She forgets the long hours waiting tables at El Sombrero to make ends meet, the tourists off the interstate giving orders like she's dumb as dirt. When a storm is on the way, she forgets Blake and Caitlin,

4

with their busy lives now in Dallas. As the clouds roll in, all her nerves begin to hum.

There is a sudden thud against the side of the house, and Jay straightens. 'What the hell?' He hates wild weather. He's told Shelley stories of running to his parents' storm cellar in the dead of the night, lashed by rain, terrified by lightning jags and crashes. He has bad memories of the cellar too, of spiderwebs and bugs as long as his boy fingers. Their cellar is much better – just a few yards from their back door, with a super-bright light and a floor Jay keeps clean enough to eat off.

'Just a pail maybe, blowin' around.' Shelley speaks lightly to hide her excitement. It's shameful, her love of storms. She knows it's wrong – she doesn't wish anyone harm. But she loves it all – the blast of wind, the dazzle of lightning, the whole-body throb of thunder.

Jay frowns. 'I can't see how there's not a warnin' already. There's a storm comin' this way for sure.' He rubs his forehead. 'Maybe we should go to the cellar, settle in.'

Shelley leans to pat Elvis, their snowy Siamese, as he winds around her legs. 'Nah, there ain't even a tornado watch.' She unplugs the laptop. 'I'll stay up, keep an eye on the website. Why don't you go on and get some more sleep? You still look beat.'

Jay sighs. 'I might just do that.' His breath is musty as he kisses her cheek. He heads back down the hall. 'Get me up if there's a change.'

In the living room, Shelley turns on the lamp and opens the curtains, but it's still too dark to see more than reflections. She curls up on the sofa, the computer in her lap. Elvis leans against her, closer than usual. Lightning spikes outside and she waits for the faraway grumble.

~

Bang! Bang-bang!

Shelley jumps, pulling out her earphones. She's been watching *2018 – A Year in Review* on the Texas Storm Chasers' YouTube channel.

Bang!

Something on the roof is slapping in the wind. Shelley's pulse leaps at the rush of air outside – constant now, like a giant leaf blower cleaning the house. She changes tabs and fear slides down her back. Almost half an hour has passed since she last checked the Storm Prediction Center site. A tornado warning is now in place for most of Castro County.

She lifts the laptop over Elvis, dumping it on the couch. The living-room windows frame a sunless morning. The wide skies are pale grey, changing to steely in the south, where the clouds are layered thick and mean. The only real tree on their ranch, the oak beside the barn, bucks in the wind. Stalks of hay fly past, loose from bales in their three-sided shed.

Jay's shirt is damp as she shakes his shoulder. 'Jay. There's a tornado warnin'.'

He throws the sheet back. 'Jesus Christ, Shelley.' Shoving his wallet and phone into a pocket, he hurries to the cupboard, pulling out a backpack. 'I'll get clothes and the safe deposit. You get the rest?'

She nods, her heartbeat thumping in her ears. The wind is louder than she's ever heard it.

In the kitchen, she grabs a hemp bag and collects crackers, bananas and two cans of beans. Just before she leaves, she spins around for the can opener.

'Come on!' Jay is at the back door, his face grim. Shelley joins him, and air swirls under the door, rising cold on her legs beneath the robe.

They burst outside and cross the lawn. The oak tree bows towards them. At the edge of the pastures behind the house, the low mesquite scrub billows and sways. The horses whinny in their barn stalls, their cries faint and panicked. The wind shoves Jay and Shelley one way then the other, and hay snags in their hair, but it takes only seconds to reach the cellar door. Jay yanks it up and they plunge down the steps, closing the door above them.

When Jay clicks the switch, the light dazzles their eyes. The shelter is small and bare, its single shelf holding a flashlight, a radio and two large bottles of water. They sit on the floor and pull stalks from each other's hair.

Shelley checks her phone for SPC updates, but the site won't load. 'There's no twister coming. They just get all riled up.' But as she says these words – words she's grumbled twice before – she doesn't believe them. Not today. Something big and brutal is coming their way.

'We forgot Elvis.'

Her husband looks at her with surprise. They are ranchers, and though they love animals they're not sentimental. Animals find their own safe places.

Shelley pictures the cat brushing past her legs. 'I need to go back real quick.'

'Okay.'

She's noticed that Jay tries not to argue these days, not since their last huge fight when she told him she was tired of this farm, tired of washing and cleaning and cooking like a slave when she could have been so much more. She bit back the rest of it – that she's restless as a fenced-in mustang. That she thinks she wants to leave.

'If you can't find him, come straight back.' Jay's forehead is creased with worry.

'I know, I know.'

The wind sucks the breath from her lungs as she heads across the lawn. It lifts her hair above her head, flips her robe like an inside-out umbrella. Shelley presses on, and a few moments later she slams inside the house, flushed and panting.

Elvis rubs along the kitchen cupboards, tail like a question mark, mournful and lost.

'Here, fella. Come to Momma.' Shelley lifts him up, nuzzling his head with her chin. She's become ridiculous about the cat, buying knitted mouse toys and a plush bed he ignores, sleeping in the armchair instead.

A series of knocks on the walls outside makes her clutch Elvis tight. The wind pounds and screams. Shelley tucks the cat inside her bathrobe, his fur soft against her chest.

With one arm around the cat, she opens the door. The force is immense, a physical blow. Elvis yowls and jumps, his claws scratching her stomach as he darts inside. The doorknob tugs in her hand, then rips from her grasp as the door flings back against the house. Her gown wrenches open.

Rain spits from a gloomy sky. Gravel fragments sting her legs and grass blows across her eyes. Shelley knows she should run for the shelter, or back to the house, but the storm clouds have joined to form a huge, dark spaceship, shifting and building. She is entranced. Lightning forks down, sizzling bright, and thunder shakes her bones.

Then she sees it, maybe a half-mile away. Like a thin, searching finger, it descends from the cloud – a long, grey funnel that sweeps the ground, tracing a careful line. She shields her eyes with her hands, ignores the bite of grit. Her hair is wet to her face and her robe flaps around her shoulders and she thinks for a moment how crazy she must look but she doesn't care, doesn't give a damn.

The tornado churns in the fields, throwing up dirt and witchgrass, the funnel turning brown and growing wider. Cattle run down a fence line as the tornado approaches, slow and majestic, tracking sideways past the house.

The turbulence fills her ears. She gazes up the whirling tube – a round, circling tower. She is breathless at the sight.

The rotation drags her body, pulls her skin and yanks her hair, and then her bathrobe rips from her body, goes flying, whisked into the air. The garment shifts and folds, as if examined by invisible hands. It spirals upwards, higher and higher, closer to the funnel, until it is sucked in and disappears. Shelley stands naked in the yard, her heart wild in her chest.

She will leave Jay. She will take the money from her stash, go to her sister's and figure out a whole new life. She will go to college, or open a florist shop. She'll travel to Africa. She will be the person she was meant to be, before she married Jay. Before she had two kids by the age of twenty. Before she got stuck in Dimmitt on a dried-out ranch.

A movement to the left catches her eye. Jay is at the storm cellar door, waving, his mouth open in a yell. His hair is blown up and his back is hunched.

She tries to run, but the wind makes her stagger. At last she stumbles down into the shelter, sitting on the bottom step as Jay bolts the door. He's staring at her and he pulls his T-shirt off, using it to dab her skin. 'What the hell, Shelley?'

She is covered in cuts from the debris, dozens of thin lines of blood, and there are small purple bruises too, all over her body. Jay opens a bottle, tips water onto his shirt and presses gently in places on her stomach, her face, her arms, her legs. She touches a few marks in awe.

When the blood is mostly cleaned, Jay passes her a flannel shirt, helps her trembling arms into the sleeves. He doesn't speak, tending to Shelley with his big calloused hands.

Finally, he sits beside her. 'Where's the cat?'

Shelley shakes her head. 'He ran back.' She wraps her arms around herself. 'He'll be okay.'

Jay's brows draw together as he looks at her, his familiar gold-brown eyes just inches away. His body is warm against her side. Above them, the storm still blares, but the noise is easing, like the volume is being slowly turned down.

'You alright, Shell?' His voice is calm, his gaze steady.

Her throat turns dry.

She remembers another day when Jay stayed calm, all those years ago, when they were teenagers. When she'd peed on the stick and there were two pink lines and she'd bawled until her eyes swelled almost shut. He'd told her it would all be okay, that he loved her and he'd love their baby and he'd take care of them always.

'Oh, Jay.'

She thinks of their quiet mornings with coffee and bacon, thinks of riding the horses under wide open skies. She pictures the grandkids that will surely come along and the Dallas trips to follow.

She inhales sharply, then exhales. The trip to Africa and the florist shop go spinning away.

She leans her head against his bulk.

Outside, the wind has died down but the rain is heavy now, beating on the cellar door. The light inside flickers off, then on again.

IF YOU'RE HAPPY

THE POMPEII NIGHTMARE HAD SPOOKED him again. Alistair sat at the table, gripping his glass in the quiet apartment. He was still caught by the dream, running down a narrow street through haze and heat, jostled by others, struggling to breathe.

Gradually he became aware of sounds – the hum of the fridge, the ticking of the clock, the drip of the tap he'd tried to fix. His back ached and he shifted on the chair. He wouldn't sleep for hours.

As he rose from the table, another noise reached his ears. He paused. Nothing.

He placed his glass in the sink, and heard it again – a faint mewling.

Alistair listened, head tilted. His brain fizzed and sparked as he crept into the living room.

There it was again. Not a cat – a child. The crying continued, drifting in through the window left ajar.

Alistair walked over, peering down. There was no one on the street, but there were cars parked on either side. He returned to the bedroom for his dressing-gown and slippers, and slid his phone and keys into his pocket.

He took the stairs; he never used the rickety lift. As he trotted down in his short pyjamas, gown flapping, he hoped he wouldn't encounter any neighbours.

When the entrance door closed behind him, he waited. The road was deserted. The air was cool but not cold – a perfect Edinburgh summer's night. He inhaled the sweet, malty scent of the city.

Then he heard it – a muffled wailing. It came from a nearby car, an old bomb with patchy paintwork. The driver's window was open an inch.

Alistair started towards the car, but his steps slowed as he approached. The streetlight fell on a baby – maybe two years old, maybe younger – strapped in a car seat. It was bawling, its face red and wet. The child's eyes widened when it saw him.

Alistair squinted up at empty windows on both sides of the street. He wondered what the hell to do. He could call the police and leave it to them, head back to the apartment. But the baby's frantic eyes pulled him in.

He glanced around. If there was a piece of wire he could unlock the car; he'd done it once with his old Mazda. There was nothing nearby, nothing in the gutters. The baby watched him, its mouth turned down in fear.

In a burst of inspiration, Alistair thought of trying the doors. The driver's door was locked, and the baby's door behind it. Around the other side, the back door was locked. With a sense of defeat, Alistair tried the passenger door. It released with a metallic scrape.

He reached to unlock the back door and opened it slowly, then placed a knee on the seat.

'Hello there.' He knew nothing about babies. You had to

have a partner first and that was one thing he could never seem to manage. The few women he'd dated always told him he was sweet, but that they liked him as a pal.

'I'm Alistair,' he said.

The child had curly blond hair and big, round eyes. It wore a pale shirt and shorts. Alistair couldn't tell if it was girl or boy.

'Where's your ma and da then?'

The baby stared, eyes brimming with tears.

Alistair continued to talk in a soothing voice, surprised at his knack for it. He was blethering away like a numpty to this kid. He leant across and unclicked the straps of the baby's seat. It shrugged its arms free but didn't get out. Perhaps it couldn't walk yet? But that wasn't right; his sister had children – grown now – and they were all walking before they'd reached this size.

'Come on, now.' He stretched out his arms.

The baby regarded him with a serious face. It hiccupped. Its mouth twisted now and then, spasms of sorrow. Finally, it turned and climbed down from the car seat, shuffling across to where Alistair waited. He lifted it to his chest, backing out of the car into the darkened street.

~

'That's it, that's the way.'

The baby was gulping milk, huge thirsty guzzles, its hair shining golden on its tilted-back head. Alistair held the tumbler, afraid the child would drop it, but its hands were strong. When all the milk was gone, Alistair set the glass on the table.

The baby sat on the chair, chubby legs extended. It gazed at Alistair.

The police had said they'd send someone within the hour. They'd taken ages to process his call, seemed tense and busy. Alistair didn't mind if they were delayed. There was a lightness inside him, a feeling of great fortune.

'Well, wee babby, what now?' he said.

Then he remembered the stuffed toy he'd been given at last year's work party – a bear in a vest, its arm tied to a toy spade. All those young people thought it was a hoot, his passion for archaeology. He couldn't help it if he got enthusiastic. Some finds were pure brilliant, like the skeletons found in last month's digs at Pompeii – ten poor souls huddled on the floor of a room, smothered by hot ash and gases. Those dafties at work didn't get it. All they cared about was their next holiday, or getting blootered on the weekends.

He moved to the hall cupboard, keeping up a constant patter.

'Here you go. *Teddy*.' He smiled, and settled the bear in the baby's lap.

The child looked down, wove its small fingers into the plush fur. After a moment, it pulled the bear closer, clutching the toy to its chest.

'Bah,' said the baby.

Was it saying 'bear'? Alistair grinned. 'Yes, *bear*. A teddy bear.'

'Bah,' the child said again, and wiped its face on the teddy, leaving a trail of snot and tears.

Alistair kept smiling. The mess didn't matter. He'd give the bear to the baby, let it take something of comfort when it left. It looked happier already, hugging the soft toy.

The apartment seemed different too. Bigger. Brighter. The walls gleamed as if freshly washed.

Alistair racked his brain for more ideas. What did babies like?

A memory popped into his head – his mother singing to him when he was small, patting her big hands to his. He still recalled the feeling of her warm, dry palms, could see her smiling eyes.

He cleared his throat. It was a long time since he'd used his singing voice. Sometimes he hummed, just under his breath, but that wasn't the same.

'If you're happy and you know it, clap your hands,' he sang.

The baby regarded him with curious eyes.

Alistair demonstrated. 'Clap, clap!'

He continued, 'If you're happy and you know it, clap your hands, clap, clap!'

The baby released the bear, eyes goggling. The teddy sagged in its lap.

Alistair was enjoying the sound of his own voice. It was quite rich – resonant even. He flapped his hands and bent his knees, bobbing to the music. 'If you're happy and you know it, then you really ought to show it, if you're happy and you know it, clap your hands!'

This time the baby's hands lifted and came together softly – not so much a clap as assuming prayer position. Alistair's throat was suddenly thick. How could anyone leave this sweet babby?

He remembered the police were coming and he was still in striped pyjamas. He scooped up the wee thing. 'Let's away down the hall,' he said in a sing-song voice. 'Off we go, off we go.' He trotted like a horse, bouncing the child in his arms.

'Alright then?' Alistair sat the baby in the centre of the double bed. It rubbed its face, the little fists twisting. With a small resigned sigh, the baby flopped down. It closed its eyes and was still.

Edging around the room, Alistair slid his comfy jeans from the chair and stepped into them. He eased a drawer open and pulled out a shirt, changing swiftly from his pyjama top. He found his cardigan and put that on too. The baby didn't move. Alistair lifted the end of the quilt and flipped it to cover the sleeping child's legs.

The baby breathed with a slight rattle, and every now and then it hiccupped. Alistair hurried to the living room and returned with a stack of sofa pillows. He placed these on the floor either side of the bed, and used the bed pillows too, like he'd seen his sister do years ago, when her children napped at his apartment. He switched off the light and turned on the bedside lamp. As he backed out of the room, he pulled the door almost closed.

~

The knock startled him from sleep. For a moment, Alistair couldn't remember why he was in the armchair, with lights blazing overhead. Then he remembered the crying, the car. The baby.

He headed for the door, was about to open it when something compelled him to duck down the hall and close the bedroom door.

He rushed back, opened wide to two police officers and a woman in plain clothing.

'Alistair McIntosh?'

'Aye, that's me.' He kept his hand on the doorknob.

'Sorry for the delay.' The female officer didn't sound sorry, just tired and curt. 'I'm Inspector Yang, this is Sergeant Gibson, and Theresa Mackie here is from Children and Families.'

Alistair nodded. He felt sick to think of these people waking the baby, taking it into the night. The child would cry its eyes out.

'So, where's the child?'

'Not here,' he blurted. 'The parents showed up, just now.'

The three at the door looked at him, their faces blank.

The woman in plain clothing frowned. 'What d'you mean? How'd they know where to come?'

Alistair could hardly hear his own reply for the rushing in his ears. 'Oh, I saw them. I was looking out.' He gestured vaguely towards the living room. 'I went down, and they took the bairn. Said they'd not been long away.'

The police officers exchanged a glance.

'They seemed well sorry. I'm sure they were okay.' Alistair had no idea what he was saying. Wherever those parents were, whatever had happened, they were unfit to raise a child. They were likely in a pub, sucking back on fags. Or perhaps the father was long gone, and the mother drugged-out on her dealer's couch. He couldn't let the baby go back.

'Right.' Inspector Yang's manner had changed completely. She looked awake and alert. 'Well, can we come in? There may be an identifying object. Something left behind – a soft toy or blanket.'

'No. No, there's nowt.' Alistair began to close the door. 'Excuse me, I've work in a few hours. Thank you.' He shut the door on their surprised faces, clicked the lock.

He stepped back several feet, his shoulders rising and falling. He waited, hoping. There was a silence from beyond the door. No sound from the baby. Alistair pictured the cops shrugging and walking away.

He thought how he could clear out the other room, paint it yellow, buy one of those racing-car beds he'd seen in The Bed Shop. Saturdays they'd visit Montgomery Street Park, the baby in a stroller, him nodding at other parents. He'd take early retirement, manage somehow. It would be grand, him and the baby.

The door shook with a volley of pounding.

'Mr McIntosh. Open up.'

Alistair's chest hurt. They were making so much noise. They'd wake the baby, and it would be frightened. He pressed a hand to his sternum, the pain growing stronger.

'Please. Just go away.'

The bashing knocks came again.

'Mr McIntosh. You need to open the door.'

He rubbed his aching chest. This wasn't right. They couldn't take his baby.

Someone shouted, 'We're coming in. Stand back!'

Alistair dropped to his knees, fell to his side. It was hard to breathe, his ribcage compressed. Was the baby awake? Was it whimpering, needing the sound of his voice to calm it down? He could sing it another song.

There was an almighty bang, then another, and the door flew back against the wall.

Alistair lay where he'd fallen. The officers hurried past him, the other woman in their wake. Everything was hazy. The pain in his chest was vicious, like a giant squeezing him between finger and thumb.

'In here!' a man's voice said.

The baby began to cry.

Alistair curled in a ball. 'Babby, don't cry,' he whispered. 'Don't cry, now.'

His eyes streamed and he gasped, he could hardly speak. 'Alistair's here.'

ALL THIS
BEAUTY

*I*F YOU LOOK WITHOUT YOUR glasses, you can *die*.' Tim presses the dark lenses to his face, elbows propped on his knees.

'Don't be silly, love. They're just to protect your eyes.' Kari is surprised at her son. He's usually such a stickler for the truth. Elise, his twin, is the fanciful one. Right now she's stretched across the tray of the ute, gazing at a ladybug on her thumb. Her hair is a tangled mess, and there's glitter on her cheek.

'Well, your eyes will die.' Tim is determined to have the last word.

Kari lets it go.

The morning light is fading, as if a storm is on the way. Not far above the horizon, the sun is dazzling gold, but its blaze is diminishing second by second. Kari twists around, knocks on the back windscreen. Her husband is still up front, the driver's door ajar.

'Leo? You coming?'

A moment later he climbs up, steps over Elise, squeezes in beside Kari. His legs are long and gangly, bent in front like a praying mantis. His rectangular eclipse glasses top off the look.

Kari smiles. 'You are rocking that eyewear.'

Leo nods gravely – trademark deadpan Leo. But there is more to his expression, an edge of sadness, and she remembers. She'd forgotten for five seconds, or even ten.

'It's going to be okay. It'll be nothing. I feel completely fine.' Saying these words she feels a surge of fear so overwhelming she looks back to the sky, to the wide expanse and waning sun. It seems she is always thrust into this role – reassuring others, making sure everyone is alright, even when she is terrified herself. Even when her own life is in question.

Leo takes her hand, squeezing tight.

Tim is watching. 'Guess what it's called if you love eclipses?' He waits half a beat, then plunges on. 'Umbraphile. Mrs Miller told us.'

Elise sits up. 'Are we umba …' She makes a windbreak with one hand for the ladybug. 'Are we that?'

Kari laughs. 'I reckon we are. We got up at five-thirty to drive here on a school day.'

Tim frowns. '*And* you made us eat muesli bars for breakfast.'

'Look!' Leo points towards the coast. From Edge Hill they have a perfect view as the moon slides further across the sun. A sliver of light remains, just a crescent.

'Wow!' Elise is finally enthralled, the ladybug forgotten.

The moon shifts a fraction and the land is thrown into a premature dusk. Gloom surrounds them. Tim shifts closer to Kari, his sweaty leg moist against her knee. Kari's breath catches in her throat and she thinks that the shadow on the X-ray can't be anything, not this far down the track, the scar near her nipple whisper-white. Even the doctor said it could be nothing, a lump in her lung that isn't cancer.

'Okay, you were right.' Leo's voice is husky and low.

'About what?'

'This *was* worth getting up for.'

She's glad then that she set the alarm, shook the twins awake and coaxed the family to the ute. The whole of North Queensland has been discussing this for months, and she worried it wouldn't live up to the hype. They've chosen the ideal spot – far from the crowded beaches packed with tourists.

The sky is navy, and the moon a black circle with a fine rim of brilliant light.

Leo still holds Kari's hand. She looks across at their children, both leaning forward, rosy lips parted. Her heart pounds like crazy. All this beauty – it's impossible, almost unbearable.

She reaches beneath her shirt, rubs the scab on her back. She thought there'd be a proper dressing, maybe even a bandage circling her chest. Instead, the doctor smoothed down a bandaid – just like the ones Kari uses for the twins' cuts and scrapes – and told her to take it off the following day.

'Yeahhhhh,' Elise says. 'This is amazing!' She turns to her parents, eyes glinting in the half-light. There is a gap in her smile where she's lost a front tooth.

Tim is focused on the spectacle, his face alive and eager. He's lost the wariness he's had since Kari's hospital visit last week.

The temperature has dropped, the morning no longer so warm, and the breeze passing over the hillside makes the hairs rise up on Kari's arms. She breathes in the damp November air, watching the strange dark disc of the moon, far away in space, sunlight blaring at the edges. She feels like she's witnessing a birth, or a miracle.

The moon seems to hover, triumphant, smothering the sun. A minute passes, then two, until at last the sun begins to push free. Light trickles back, bathing the hillside and Cairns airport below them, flooding across the ocean.

'Is it over now?' Tim walks to the edge and jumps to the ground. 'I'm hungry.'

Kari finds she is trembling. Leo kisses her cheek and clambers down to join their son.

'Almost over. Keep your glasses on,' Leo tells Tim.

'Can we get Macca's on the way home?' Elise asks, still staring out towards the sea.

'Sure,' Kari says, just as Leo says, 'Not today.'

~

The room has slowly emptied in the two hours they've been waiting. Kari's glad the twins are at school, not whining and squirming on these hard plastic chairs. Even Leo has been up and down to the snack machine and water fountain, and is now reading a poster titled 'Healthy Bladder, Healthy You'.

In the quiet room, Kari can hear the conversation between the two receptionists. They're discussing whether the blonde one should leave her boyfriend. He smokes pot all day and is useless in bed. Despite nerves and the sick feeling in her gut, Kari wants to interrupt, wants to tell the blonde to run a mile.

'Did you at least watch the eclipse?' the brunette says.

'Nah, Brody wanted to sleep in.' The blonde receptionist looks wistful, and Kari hopes she's reaching a decision.

Leo has picked up a brochure and is examining it closely, his long neck bent to the page. Kari pictures him alone in their weatherboard house, cooking stir-fry for the children night after night, her roasting pans rusting in the cupboard.

A door into the waiting room opens and her doctor stands there, a cream-coloured chart tucked against his chest.

'Kari Wetherill.'

He's smiling, but then Dr Chandra always smiles in greeting; he smiled the day he called her in and told her the news.

'Leo,' Kari says, but she didn't need to, he's there by her side. They don't look at each other; it's all Kari can do to smile back at the doctor.

'Hello, Dr Chandra, how are you?'

'Very well, thank you, Kari.' He gestures to the cramped consulting room. It is as bleakly beige as ever, nothing on the wall except a calendar without pictures.

Kari and Leo step inside and sit on more plastic chairs. Kari closes her eyes, struggles for control. Leo's hand is on her knee, clutching her as if his grasp will keep her on this earth.

When she opens her eyes, Dr Chandra is at his desk with the chart angled towards them. He's displaying a page with his beautiful, neat-nailed hand. The biopsy results. Kari can hardly breathe, can't read the text.

Dr Chandra isn't smiling but he's sitting forward in his chair. His eyes are bright, and his face reminds her of Tim's the day before, watching the eclipse.

'The shadow is nothing, Kari. It's just a lymph node.'

The air returns to Kari's lungs and the drab room fills with light.

Leo's fingers relax on her leg. He stands to shake the doctor's hand. 'Thank you.'

Kari's gaze finds the calendar – the strips of torn-out pages, the grid of November days. Soon it will be Christmas. There is so much ahead, now. Months stretching into years.

Leo says, 'You ready, hon?' and Kari turns to him in wonder. She rises slowly to her feet.

DESCENT

HIS DAD WOULD NOT STOP talking. Even as they strode up the leaf-scattered path, he kept on blabbing. Crap about aerobic fitness and muscle mass. Dylan watched his father's calves flex and relax below the black Nike shorts. More words came flying back – *Pace. Lungs. Workout.* It was always about the workout.

Dylan checked for Emmy and Talitha. His half-sister pranced along a few metres behind, and his stepmother followed. Spotting a fresh audience, Emmy jumped towards him like a rabbit, her small hands held like paws.

Dylan lifted an arm, dangling an invisible object. 'Hey, bunny, want a carrot?'

Emmy bounced faster, giggling.

Talitha laughed too, her teeth white in her tanned face. 'You're a goose, Miss Em.' She circled her daughter's slight body and kissed the side of her face.

Talitha was so different to Dylan's steady, earnest mother that he'd been wary at first. He'd watched his dad's new wife closely, looking for signs that her cheerfulness was fake. But when he stayed over, she was the same the next day. And the next fortnight, and two weeks after that, until years had passed and his doubts were long gone.

'I'm not a goose, I'm a *rabbit!*' Emmy wriggled in her mother's arms.

'Well off you go then, rabbit.' Talitha kissed her once more before letting her go.

Dylan gave a thumbs up to Emmy and turned back to the path as it narrowed and grew steeper. The rainforest pressed close, dripping on his arms. Ferns swayed and nodded beneath the trees.

A violent scuffling nearby made him jump – just a brush turkey, scratching in the leaves.

His father paused several metres ahead. 'How's everyone doing?' he yelled. The backpack with their supplies appeared weightless on his rod-straight back. 'Are we smashing it?'

Dylan pushed wet hair off his forehead. He wasn't feeling so great. Hiking was for athletes. He pictured his electric guitar, propped in the corner of his bedroom, and ran his left thumb across the calloused tips of his fingers. He'd been practising more lately – chords, fretwork, sidestepping. He hated the school bands – he'd quit bow-tied Mr Fryer's jazz ensemble last year – but some older kids were forming an indie band and he planned to try out.

'Yep.' His voice came out deep, thank god. Now and then it still squeaked. 'All good here.' He tried to sound positive. His dad was into positive.

Bobbing up beside him, Emmy cupped her hands around her mouth. 'We are *totally* smashing it!'

Talitha called, 'We're great, Steve!'

His father made a megaphone with his own hands. 'Awesome!'

Dylan hitched up his jeans and kept walking.

~

Halfway up the mountain, his head was aching, and his breakfast Nutri-Grain bobbed in his guts. His friend Jake had brought a few beers over the night before; Jake said his parents had so much booze they'd never notice it was gone. When Dylan's mum had switched off her reading light, Dylan and Jake had sprawled on the patchy back lawn drinking lukewarm Tooheys and sniggering at the stars. Now he was paying for it.

'So.' Steve was still yapping, ploughing on uphill. 'Any … chicks … scene?'

Dylan was sweating rivers. His stomach churned and he had a desperate urge to sit down. How could his dad talk and hike in this November heat?

'Nuh. No chicks.'

'What? By … time … your age … six!'

Dylan had heard it all before – how his dad had been a player right from his teens, dating a stream of girls until the day he met Dylan's mother. And even then, Dylan had recently found out, it wasn't long after the wedding that his dad discovered girlfriends again – except these ones were on the side. Like salad, or chips.

'Yeah, well.' Dylan concentrated on placing one foot in front of the other, willing the nausea away. 'I guess I'm not you, Dad.'

They entered a clearing where a platform jutted from the hillside, peering out over the valley. Steve sprang up the steps, throwing his arms wide. 'Look at that view!'

Dylan's mouth flooded with saliva and acid snaked into his throat.

Emmy skipped up to the lookout, and Talitha joined them, lean and leggy in her cycle pants and singlet. His father's strong brown arms wrapped around his wife and child, and even from the back they were picture perfect.

Dylan ducked behind a clump of tree ferns, releasing his breakfast onto the moss-covered ground.

~

'Hang on, guys. What's this about?' Dylan examined the faded notice. His dad and Talitha didn't stop to read signs.

They had nearly reached the summit – just four hundred metres of rock scramble and they'd be there. Dylan was feeling much better, the wind here cooling his skin and drying his sweat-damp clothes. The vegemite sandwich he'd forced down ten minutes ago was finally kicking in.

'Come on, mate. You're holding up the pack.' His father smiled, but his eyes were impatient.

'Hang on, Dad. I'm just reading.' Dylan studied the sign, taking his time. He was fifteen – he wasn't that little kid, hurrying to tie his laces while his father frowned and huffed. The man could learn to *wait*. 'It says ... this mountain, Wollumbin, has spiritual meaning for the Bundjalung people. They ask visitors not to climb it.'

Stomping over, Steve read the board, folding his arms. 'They tell us this now, when we're almost at the top?'

Talitha and Emmy wandered closer. Talitha rubbed the corners of her mouth with finger and thumb. 'There were a bunch of signs back at the car park. We only looked at the map.' She tucked a hand into her husband's pretzelled arms. 'What do you think?'

Steve pulled away sharply. 'What do I think? I say we go to the top. We didn't come all this way for nothing!'

Talitha smoothed Emmy's hair, pushing loose strands behind her daughter's ears. 'Hon, I was just asking. If you want to climb, let's climb.'

His father stood taller. 'We're just walking. We're not disturbing the land. Who's coming?'

'I am!' Emmy reached up to high-five her father.

Talitha nodded. 'Sure, let's do it.' His father and Talitha slapped hands too.

The three of them looked at Dylan.

'How about you, Squib?'

It had been a long time since his dad had used that nickname. He imagined the friendly sting of his father's hand.

'I'll head back down. See you at the car.' Dylan tugged the brim of his cap.

His dad and stepmum exchanged a look.

'Why don't you take Emmy, get a head start. I'll catch you soon.' Steve patted his wife's shoulder. Talitha and Emmy began to pick their way up the rocks.

Dylan gathered his anger, ready to let fly. He had a right to go back. They were on sacred land, crashing around like dickheads. But when his father turned, the furrows in his cheeks looked deeper than before and he gazed off towards the coastline.

'You sick of me? Had enough for one day?'

Dylan exhaled slowly. 'No, Dad. It's not that.'

'I hope not. I thought we were getting on better.'

'We are. It's fine, Dad.'

'I know it's been hard for you. Especially lately.' Steve brushed at a streak of dirt on his knee. 'I never wanted you to find out all that stuff.' He straightened. 'I really messed up. But we were wrong for each other, your mum and me.'

Dylan nodded, because when he thought about it now he agreed. His mum was great but she was quiet and reserved. His dad was the opposite, seeking people and action and attention.

35

It seemed crazy they'd once been married, hard to even recall. His memories of them together were like strands of mist, disappearing when he reached for them.

'I know, Dad. It's okay. You're both happier now.' He had a flash of his mum's tired face the night before, opening bills in the tiny kitchen. He pushed the image away.

Emmy and Talitha were making good progress, clambering up with agile, sure steps.

'I'm a lucky man.' His father's voice was low and his eyes shone.

Dylan felt that familiar tug, that same gaping love. 'You should go with them, Dad. I'll see you back at the car.'

'Okay.' His dad began to climb, more slowly than before. He veered away from the safety chains, instead wedging his feet into cracks, his broad hands finding ridges, moving steadily upwards.

~

Lightning brought the climbers down in swarms. Dylan watched from the covered picnic table as they rushed from the slopes – tight-faced fathers, worried mothers and frightened kids. Only a few older teenagers strolled back to their car. Finally, he spotted his father, stepmum and sister. The three of them were laughing, and Emmy was talking a mile a minute. Dylan grinned.

He met them at the Land Rover just as the rain began – fat, heavy drops that splashed his face and ran down his neck.

Inside the car it was warm and clammy. Emmy shrieked in excitement as rain pounded on metal and thunder echoed around. Dylan widened his eyes and his sister smirked, her wet hands knotted together. Every few seconds the gloom was sliced by searing white.

'Well, I guess we're not having a picnic.' Talitha chuckled as she dried her face with a towel. They sat staring at the water-blurred windscreen.

'Oh well. We'll get home early.' Steve pulled off his cap and tossed it on the seat between Dylan and Emmy. 'I might head to the gym, pump some weights.'

'Oh, hon, again?' Talitha touched her husband's leg. 'Dylan's here.'

Steve shrugged and pressed the ignition. 'He can come too. He might like it.' The Land Rover roared into life and air conditioning blasted through the vents. Dylan shivered.

~

On the way home, Emmy fell asleep in her booster seat, her neck at a crazy angle. Dylan leant across with her balled-up jumper and gently propped her head.

'Well, that's Mount Warning done.' Steve gave Talitha's ponytail a flick as he drove.

Wollumbin, Dylan corrected in his head.

'Yep. Another mountain in the bag.' Talitha swivelled in her seat, peering around at her daughter. 'Aw, look at Emmy. She's had it!'

His father checked the back seat. 'Not bad for six, though, going all that way.' His face was tender.

'How are you feeling?' Talitha held out a bag of fruit.

'Good, thanks.' Dylan accepted an apple and took a cracking bite. Emmy muttered and shifted in her sleep, then was quiet.

'Next family outing, we should all go bowling!' His stepmother polished an apple on her shirt. 'Emmy missed you guys when we went last month. It wasn't the same, just her and me.'

Dylan swallowed his mouthful, frowning. 'What? When was this?'

His mind jumped back a few weeks. He recalled his father's weary voice, cancelling the family day out, saying he had the flu.

In the rear-view mirror, his father's gaze met Dylan's.

'You know, last month. You had that jazz band competition.' Talitha turned. 'Your dad didn't think Emmy would sit through it. Which is probably true. But he told me all about it. Said you were brilliant.'

Dylan's vision wavered, and the sounds around him became muffled.

He stared at his father's wide shoulders in that stupid, too-tight black shirt. He remembered long-ago rides on those shoulders – half-thrilled, half-panicked, gripping his dad's forehead with fingers like claws. Raised high above the world, never quite sure he was safe, heart full to bursting.

Steve spoke loudly above the rumble of the road. 'Well, my big kid needs time too. Father–son bonding. Right, Dylan?'

In the mirror his father watched and waited.

CONSTANT SMALL ADJUSTMENTS

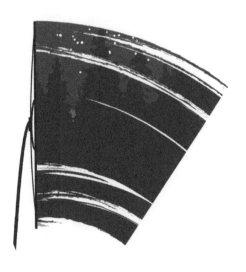

THE NOISES STARTED UP AGAIN somewhere close by – tiny scratchings, claws on wood. Noah lay turned away, snoring softly. Our whole marriage he'd slept deeply, hardly moving all night.

A scurrying echoed in the wall near my head. I wondered if the rats would be lured by the traps in the roof, the 'humane' killing option our twelve-year-old had argued for – plastic tunnels fitted with tight rubber bands that snapped around a rodent's neck. Pretty gruesome, but poison was worse. Our son had read an article about rats bleeding to death over days. And snap traps could catch just a nose, causing slow, agonised starvation. I'd bought two strangle traps at Bunnings and baited them with peanuts.

There was a pause, silence in the darkness. I pressed the mobile on my bedside table – it was after two, and my eyes were dry and sore.

Noah hadn't stirred. He came home from building sites dusty and weary, ready for sleep. Not edgy and tense the way I was, the way so many cops were by the end of a shift. The truth was, since the call-out last Christmas Eve, I'd been more than just edgy.

From the ceiling came sudden scrambling, a squeak. I stiffened. A rat in a trap? Was it even now fighting for air, its tiny paws scraping at its throat? I strained to listen, but all I could hear was the swish of my heartbeat.

Something scuffled, stopped. I imagined the rat's final gasps.

Noah's breathing was quiet now. He was innocent – no horrors in his head, no guilt to disturb his sleep. A car passed by, headlights strobing our curtains. I wondered if I'd ever sleep well again.

A whimpering came from the roof. I pictured a rat bowed over the corpse of another, the ligature tight around its dead mate's neck. Did rats mourn each other's deaths?

The cries grew louder, and I couldn't believe Noah still slept; though a heavy sleeper, he'd always woken at sounds of distress, getting up to our kids in the night.

The crying was awful, like all the sadness I'd ever heard in my life. I turned on my side, pulled the pillow over my head.

~

By the start of late shift the next day, I was exhausted. At least the station was quiet, the usual afternoon lull. I headed to the staffroom for coffee.

Marc smiled as I walked past, his lips stretched upwards for too long. I nodded and kept going. I had to talk to him alone, begin to put things right. At my desk, I clutched my mug, planning what I'd say. But before I'd finished my coffee, the receptionist put through a call.

It wasn't like the call last December – the person of concern was elderly, in a different situation. But there were similarities. The caller was a woman, maybe fortyish, the same blend of guilt and worry in her voice. As I listened I began to sweat. I knew Marc and I should go. I promised we'd check it out, waved Marc over and filled him in as we drove away.

Even before I pulled to the kerb, my hands trembled on the wheel. The street looked innocent enough – hedges and freshly painted fences – but I'd thought that last time. Marc watched me undo my seatbelt and I wanted to snap at him, tell him to shut up though he hadn't opened his mouth.

Afternoon light filtered through trees. Somewhere in the distance, children yelled and laughed. I thought about my two boys, at home by now with Noah, eating toasted sandwiches and drinking their milk.

'You don't have to do this. It's just an old man. Probably forgotten his hearing aids. You wait here and I'll check things out.' Marc's hands were spread calm and confident on his thighs. His wedding band caught the sun, flashing gold.

I twisted my own dull band. I needed to prove I was still good at my job – at least doing one thing right. *With honour we serve.*

My tongue was thick and dry. 'I'll be fine.' I opened the door and stepped out.

The urge to stay with the patrol car was strong. I would have welcomed a drunk and disorderly, a public nuisance, a theft. Almost anything but this. Marc stood waiting, hand on the car. He'd been with me that December day. He knew what I'd seen, had seen it too.

I'd found the man hanging in a leopard tree. His bare feet had dangled a metre from the ground, pale below his jeans. He'd glared down at me with swollen, angry eyes.

You're too late, his eyes had said.

I shut the car door. 'Come on then.' I started up the concrete path, Marc behind me.

A sudden bang made me swivel.

A few houses down, a four-wheel drive had reversed into a hatchback. The tiny car was pushed to the far side of the road, the driver leaping out already, her voice a screech.

'You idiot! Did you even look?'

Marc shook his head. 'Bloody hell.' He gestured to the accident. 'How about you sort that, I'll check the old guy.' He'd been doing this a lot – acting as if he was senior constable. Maybe it was instinct, like when one animal knows another is wounded.

'No thanks. You deal with that, I'll head in here.'

His eyes met mine and I felt that jolt, that fierce connection. It was wrong, what we were doing. It made me sick when I thought about Noah finding out. But only Marc understood. Only he knew the hanging man's accusing face. The acrid smell of the man's wet jeans. The words in the note, left for his daughter.

'Are you sure, Lin?'

The way Marc said my name – soft and tender – made me angry again.

'Absolutely. See you in five.'

~

As I waited outside the front door, images began to flicker in my mind – the same horror slideshow. Every time the pictures disappeared – sometimes for a whole day – I hoped they might be gone. They always returned.

The doorbell melody faded. I tried to calm myself. *It won't be like last time, this is an old man – he just hasn't heard the phone.* I pressed the bell again, remembering the daughter calling from

Melbourne: 'He hasn't answered all day.' I gave up waiting and stepped to the wide front window.

At first, all I could see was my own grim face reflected in the glass. Leaning forward, I cupped my hands to the window. Inside was a neat living room, and further back a dining room. Nothing looked out of place. I pushed off the glass, leaving two curved smears.

A pair of noisy miners scuffled on the roof. Down the road, Marc stood talking on the footpath, pen and notepad in hand. A tow truck ground to a halt on the far side of the Range Rover, yellow lights spinning – a true first responder, like Marc always joked.

I swallowed back sourness. Unlatching the side gate, I walked around the lowset brick home, calling as I went. 'Hello? Ted? *Hello?*'

Through the dining-room window, the kitchen looked tidy. A few cups and plates sat in the dish rack.

'Ted? It's the police.'

Even before that December day, I'd hated welfare checks. Over the years, I'd found people half-naked, injured, semiconscious and deceased. People who'd died in their sleep, or after a fall. A few from overdoses. But before December, not a hanging.

'Ted? Hello?' I turned onto the back terrace, my heart pounding like a warning.

I tried to keep the visions at bay, but it was no use. I saw the bulging eyes, the purple face, the pointed toes. There was no air; my lungs weren't working. I staggered towards a pair of chairs, collapsing onto the closest one.

Gradually I slowed my breathing. Lifting my head, I glanced around for distraction.

Sturdy garden beds ran down the fence lines each side. Fruit trees clustered near the back. On a grevillea by the terrace, a pale-green butterfly sat fanning its wings. I'd read somewhere during my insomnia bouts that this was how butterflies kept their temperature stable. Wings in to cool down, wings out to warm up. Constant small adjustments to maintain a steady state. The butterfly spread its wings wide, paused in the sunshine, then flitted away.

Pushing to my feet, I trod past tomato bushes and bean plants to the tiny orchard. A glimpse of blue made me inhale. A figure was slumped forward at the base of a tree.

I couldn't approach the body, couldn't step closer. I fumbled for my radio. Shaking, I raised the handset. Then the shape moved. A grey head appeared. An arm made circling motions on the ground.

I replaced the handset.

'Ted? Ted Armstrong?'

The head popped up higher, turning stiffly my way.

I wobbled between two lemon trees laden with fruit.

'Senior Constable Lindsay Draper.' My voice quavered, and heat rushed to my cheeks.

The old man sat on his haunches, brushing dirt-stained hands on his trousers. His forehead creased above woolly eyebrows. 'Is everything alright? My family?'

I nodded. 'Yes. They're fine. Your daughter ... was just ... worried about you.' I struggled to force out the words. A concerned caller, just like on Christmas Eve, except then it was the woman whose ex-husband hadn't shown to collect their daughter.

The dead man filled my vision. My chest heaved. I heard myself making gulping sounds.

Ted stood slowly. He was tall and wiry, his clothing loose on his frame. His weathered face was patterned with shade.

'I've been spreading mulch,' he said. He gestured to the ground below the lemon trees. 'Wonderful stuff, eh? The way it draws water in and keeps weeds out.'

There was a musty, earthy tang in the air. I wiped my face on my shoulder.

'I often have a cuppa this time of day. I drink it up there, looking over the garden.' Ted pointed to the pair of chairs. 'I'll bring some out.' He trudged towards the house.

~

The cup was clean. Sometimes I was offered tea and the cup was stained, or spotted with substances unknown. I cradled my drink. The tea was hot and strong.

Ted passed the gingernuts and I took another one.

My radio crackled with Marc's voice. I picked up. 'Yep?'

'Lin, you okay? This is almost sorted, just a bit of drama. Turns out Range Rover dude is unlicensed – DUI.'

'Yep, all good here. Ted was spreading mulch.' I raised my eyebrows at Ted.

'Righto. See you soon.'

I hooked the radio back into my vest, turning to the old man. 'About before, I—'

Ted waved a hand. 'You're fine.'

A Monarch butterfly flitted to the grevillea. It sat on a flower, displaying its wings. They reminded me of stained-glass windows – the orange so vivid, framed in black.

'My wife loved butterflies. She planted that grevillea to attract them.'

Ted crunched through biscuits and refilled our cups. The yard was warm, no trace of a breeze. A plane hummed far above us, where puffs of cloud drifted through the sky. The butterfly still posed, dipping its head, shifting its wings.

'Here you are. I was buzzing for ages!' Marc appeared around the corner with his easy swagger, his voice strangely loud in the hush. His face had a slight end-of-day sheen that I knew would taste of salt.

'I told you Ted was mulching. Not really an indoor thing,' I said. Marc was so young, so brash.

Ted smiled at my partner. 'Hello, officer. Ted Armstrong.' He rose from the chair, holding out a hand. I stood too.

Marc shook the old man's hand, the muscles in his tanned arm flexing.

'Yeah, hi. Marc Papadopoulos. Constable.'

Ted released his grasp and hitched up his trousers. 'Thank you both for coming by. I'm sorry for any trouble.' He turned to me. 'And thank you for staying for a cuppa.'

I took his hand, felt his bones so close to the skin.

~

When we parked at the station, I cut the engine but didn't get out.

Marc looked over. He knew me too well.

'So that's it then? You get back on the horse and you ditch me?' His eyes glittered in the shadows of the car.

I focused on my wedding ring, its solid width, as I gripped the wheel.

'Marc. We can't keep doing this. It's not fair on anyone.'

Marc sighed. 'Yeah.' He shifted in his seat. 'Yeah, I know.'

I watched a car pull in and park a few spaces down. 'I'll apply for a transfer tomorrow.'

For a long time Marc didn't reply. When he spoke again, he used a voice so low I had to strain my ears, like listening for the rats.

'I'll miss you, Lin.'

~

I shed my uniform and bra in the bathroom and crept into the darkened bedroom. Groping under the pillow, I found my T-shirt, pulled it on, and eased into bed. Noah was motionless beside me.

A half-mile away, the midnight goods train squealed as it curved around the bend. Noah breathed evenly, in and out. I laid a hand lightly on his chest, felt it rise and fall.

Tears welled in my eyes. I couldn't see his face, but I knew every contour.

'Can't sleep?'

I lifted my head. 'Sorry. I woke you.'

'I don't mind.' He wrapped an arm across mine, pulling me close.

My tears leaked onto his T-shirt and I wondered if he'd feel them.

'Noah?'

He rubbed my arm. 'Yeah?' He still sounded half asleep. His heartbeat was slow and strong.

Words piled like stones in my mouth.

He nudged me. 'You still awake?'

I had to speak, had to say it.

'I can't hear the rats anymore.' I wiped my cheeks in the dark. 'I've been lying here for ages. Haven't heard a thing.'

Noah kissed my forehead. 'Well, maybe there were only two. I'll check the traps tomorrow.'

'Thank you.' I pulled his hand to my mouth and kissed his fingers. They were big and rough-skinned, same as they'd been when we met at twenty.

We lay together and the house creaked around us. One of our boys muttered in his sleep. A dog barked then went silent. Noah's breathing changed, grew heavy.

All the noises merged together, small beloved sounds. I relaxed against Noah and the room slipped away.

I saw orange wings, fanning wide.

A SHIFT IN
THE ICE

JOSEPH CHEWED A MOUTHFUL OF tepid poached egg. There was no one else down this end of the room, and he gazed out the long windows to sunny grasslands and the mountains of Vatnajökull National Park.

'Well, hi again! Joe, right?'

It was that American woman, in another lurid tracksuit. She huffed into the chair opposite, her plate piled with eggs and bacon, topped with two slices of thickly buttered toast.

He nodded. 'Joseph.'

'I knew it was Joe! I've got a good memory for names; tell me once and I remember forever.' She batted her mascaraed lashes. 'Remember mine?'

He picked up his knife and fork. 'Sorry, I don't.' He sliced the second poached egg sharply through the middle. It was firm, like cheese.

'I'm Kimberly! Remember now?'

Joseph forced his face into what he hoped was a friendly expression. 'Oh, right. Yes. Kimberly.'

'But you can call me Kimmy.' The woman lifted the salt

shaker, her hand rising and falling as she circled the plate, a blizzard falling softly on her food.

Joseph thought of the low-salt, high-fibre foods Aden always bought before he got sick. How Aden cooked most nights, though both of them worked. How he'd sit on the benchtop in their Sydney flat, drying up as Joseph washed the pots and pans.

Joseph pushed the cold egg away. 'Well, have a good day.'

'Thanks, Joe, you too. Now don't forget – it's Kimmy!' She waved with her fork.

He blinked. 'Kimmy. Got it.' He strode out and down the hallway to his faux-wood-panelled room. Crawling across crumpled sheets, he pushed his head beneath the pillow. There was a roar in his throat, a raving scream. He gulped and breathed until the moment passed and all that remained was the same coiled tightness that had been there for months.

~

He'd mentioned travel to a few select people as they picked at mini sliders and sipped riesling at the wake. Friends with furrowed brows told him yes, of course – he should go somewhere warm, what about Fiji? His sister Winnie smiled vaguely as she counted hired glassware. Later that evening on the phone from Brisbane, his father grunted and said, 'What about the firm?' Joseph hauled his temper back, told his father that the firm could cope for two weeks, or they could find another lawyer.

Winnie had tried to stay over, but he'd sent her away and slumped on the couch, finally alone. He'd opened a bottle of Glenfiddich given to Aden by an old boyfriend way too late, when Aden's swallow was no longer 'safe', as the speech pathologist said, as if his throat might be hiding a tiny weapon, a gun or a knife.

By then the motor neurone disease was in its final stages, and he could drink only thickened fluids – viscous slimes that would slide down without choking him.

That night, Joseph had sipped Scotch and watched TV, ads and all, something he hadn't done for years – not since he and Aden started on box sets and Netflix. His mind glazed over, and his lips buzzed against the glass and it was the best he'd felt since that sickening moment when Aden hadn't breathed in.

At eleven o'clock, a late movie came on – *The Secret Life of Walter Mitty*. Ben Stiller was chasing Sean Penn for reasons Joseph couldn't discern, but the scenery was stunning. Snow-capped mountains swept down to green meadows, fishing villages and pebbly beaches. It was like nothing he'd seen before. He sat forward, his heart huge in his chest. He would go to Iceland.

~

Joseph stepped from foot to foot, watching through the foyer windows for the minibus. The *Explore Iceland* website promised the four-hour hike along the Svínafellsjökull glacier would be the experience of a lifetime. At least he'd be outdoors, there'd be fresh air. The disinfectant smell would clear from his nostrils. And the ball of wire in his neck might finally unwind.

A white van with grit-covered panels rolled to a stop in front of the hotel and Joseph headed into the chill morning air.

'Wait for me!' Kimmy rushed up in a pink puffer vest, her cheeks bright with rouge and her mouth freshly painted since breakfast.

Joseph froze, holding the door as she hustled by.

'This is gonna be awesome!' She smiled as she hoisted herself into the bus, waving long-nailed fingers at the other passengers. 'Hi, y'all! I'm Kimmy and this is Joe.'

A few gave muted greetings, eyeing them both. A blonde woman next to the driver began to speak.

'Hi Kimmy, hi Joe, welcome to the Glacier Quest tour. I'm Birta and I'll be your guide today.' Her spiel had the plastic sound of repetition. 'Take a seat and we'll head up to the icefields.'

Kimmy settled herself by a window and Joseph surveyed his options – a seat beside Kimmy, or next to a scowling teen. He edged in beside the American woman, careful not to touch any part of her, his leg propped in the aisle.

'Well this is cosy.' Kimmy nudged him.

He stared past her, out the window. The summer tundra was a rich green, dotted with tiny wildflowers.

'Ain't it beautiful?' She pulled out a piece of gum, popped it in her mouth.

'Mmm.' He kept his gaze trained on the landscape as her large, inquisitive eyes swivelled his way.

Birta's patter about the region kept Kimmy quiet until they reached the Explore Iceland hut at Skaftafell.

'Well I'm real excited. I've never seen a glacier. Never been outside Texas, truth be told.' She followed Joseph from the minibus, lining up with the others as Birta passed out crampons.

Kimmy sat down next to Joseph, and they tried their spikes on for size. 'How 'bout you, Joe? You excited?'

He kicked off his crampons and zipped up his windcheater. It was a fine morning, but the breeze was cool. 'Oh yeah,' he muttered.

'What's that?' Kimmy leant closer, her perfume wafting up his nose, pungent and sweet.

Birta clapped her hands together and all chatter died away.

'Here, it is possible to see the effect of climate change. In just twenty years, the glacier has retreated nine hundred metres. So now we must walk further from the car park. We'll stop before the ice.'

The group followed her, crampons clanking like cutlery.

Joseph fell in behind. A bird flitted past and the sun warmed his hair. The sparkling glacier lay just ahead, pouring down from mountain to valley. His irritation began to dissipate. This was what he had hoped for – to walk in another land, to forget himself, to forget everything.

But not far in front, a pink figure waited.

'Joe! So sorry, I just went chargin' ahead.' Kimmy tucked a hand around his arm. Joseph glanced at her sharply, but the next instant she'd released him, listening to Birta, who was handing out icepicks from her backpack.

'So now we are at Svínafellsjökull glacier. Put on your spikes and take a pick to keep your balance. Then please follow me and walk where I walk.' The guide looked intently at each of them. 'If you take another way, you may fall into a crack, or in a stream, or even down the mountain. You must follow my tracks, yes?'

There were murmurs of obedience as they bent to their boots, then the group trailed after Birta in single file, hiking in the high-stepping style she demonstrated. Joseph dropped behind Kimmy, concentrating on placing his feet. His new hiking boots were rubbing his heels.

'Well ain't this just spectacular!' Kimmy breathed. She kept stopping to comment, and each time he was forced to halt abruptly. He tried not replying, hoping she'd give up, but she was undeterred. Blood pounded in his ears and he stabbed at raised knolls of ice with his icepick as they passed.

The gradient of their climb was gentle, zigzagging across,

but Birta set a brisk pace. Though Kimmy seemed unaffected, churning uphill while offering random thoughts, Joseph grew breathless. He recalled the 'moderate' rating of the climb with unease. He hadn't exercised for months.

The sun glinted off every surface and even through sunglasses the light hurt his eyes. The mountain peak grew closer.

'Sweet Jesus, look at that!' Kimmy planted her feet wide without warning and Joseph pulled up sharply. She pointed to a crack in the ice a few metres from the path. The dark depth of it sent a cold finger down Joseph's back. He imagined tumbling into the void.

'Yep. A crevasse.'

He said nothing more. Kimmy moved on.

The wind had died down and he was boiling in his jacket. He stopped to peel it off and Kimmy waited.

'If you tie it round your waist …' She reached around his body and he twitched away.

'It's okay, I can fix my own clothes.'

Kimmy nodded, took a step back. 'You know who you remind me of? My husband, Terry. I drove him nuts sometimes, but he was a good man.' Her eyes were shinier than before.

Joseph was aware he should feel some sympathy for Kimmy, maybe even a kinship. It seemed Terry was no longer on the scene – probably a heart attack, all that bacon. But Joseph felt nothing. He was just hot, and his heels were throbbing.

They rose higher. The vista opened to the wide expanse of mountain, split by the tongue of blue-white ice. Above the crunch of boots on snow was the rush of water, deep within the glacier. Clear mountain rivulets trickled between folds and shallow puddles pooled on the ice. He wondered if the glacier was stable. It seemed to be melting before his eyes.

Even without his jacket he was too warm, and sweat prickled the back of his neck. He stopped to unwind his scarf and shove it in his pocket.

When he looked up, the rest of the group was a long way ahead. He felt less puffed, but when he tried to pick up the pace, Kimmy was right there.

'We should catch up to the others.'

'What's that, Joe?'

'We should hurry up.'

Kimmy looked back. 'Aw, honey. It's gonna be just fine. They won't leave us behind.' Her smile made him livid.

He tried to edge around her, but their course had narrowed. To the right, there was a long, narrow puddle and a dip in the ice before the glacier rose up again. To their left, the glacier sloped steeply away.

He walked at her right elbow, biding his time.

'There's no rush. They'll wait for us.' Kimmy kept walking at her same infuriating pace.

Maybe Terry wasn't dead after all; maybe poor old Terry had just made a run for it.

Watching her over-sprayed hair bob up and down was making his jaw clench.

'Move. Out. Of. My. Way.' He growled the words at Kimmy's broad back.

'What?' She turned, her eyes wide.

'Let. Me. Past.' His arms shook with rage, the icepick trembling by his side.

Kimmy's face was white. 'Joe. Please don't.' She stumbled backwards along the path.

He followed her. 'Stop!' She was acting ridiculous; he just wanted to go by. He raised his arms high, yelled, 'Just stop!'

But already she was falling.

~

Kimmy lay still. A cavern like a small room had cracked open where the puddle had been. Her body was splayed across the icy floor, one leg twisted awkwardly beneath her.

Joseph's icepick dropped beside him. 'Kimmy! Are you alright?'

He knelt at the edge. He could see no movement – no rise and fall of breathing. His neck was clammy where the sweat had chilled.

Then Kimmy whimpered, and shifted. She rose slowly to her knees, her clothing darkly sodden.

'Oh God, I'm sorry, I'm so sorry.' He shook his head. 'I just …'

Kimmy struggled to her feet, then fell back in the slush with a cry, clutching her ankle. He turned to clamber down but she held up her hand. 'No! Don't come near me!'

He stopped. 'I won't hurt you. I was never going to hurt you.'

The sun had dimmed, a bank of dirty clouds spread across the sky. A cold breeze ruffled Joseph's hair. Kimmy sat in the hollow, her leg straightened in front. She wiped her nose, her eyes ringed with mascara. 'What the hell is wrong with you?'

He had no answer; there was nothing that truly made sense.

'I don't know.' He rubbed his forehead. 'I've been pretty angry.'

Joseph stood, scanning the glacier until his gaze snagged on the blue of Birta's jacket.

Birta waved from across the ice and he made large scooping gestures, summoning her back. She stopped waving, but the group didn't move.

Kimmy dug out a tissue and blew her nose. 'Sure seems that way.'

Without sunshine, the temperature was dropping. Joseph pocketed his Ray-Bans and wound his scarf around his neck. He climbed down the sloped wall of the cavern until he stood beside Kimmy. This time she made no objection as he helped her up to the path, then lowered her gently.

She shivered in violent waves, her face pinched. 'My ankle's bad. I think it might be broken.'

Joseph offered his hand. 'Lean on me. I'll take you to the others.'

Kimmy's big, dark eyes snapped onto his. 'Well bless your heart, Joe, I thought you were smart.' She ignored his outstretched arm. 'I ain't goin' nowhere 'cept back the way we came.'

The sky was steely grey. The wind was picking up, hunting across the frozen surface. Birta and the others weren't any closer, but they'd gathered in a cluster.

'Well alright then.' He sat with his back to hers, facing the wind, protecting her from the brunt of it. 'We can wait for them here.' His eyes stung and his toes were icy.

Kimmy shifted so their shoulders pressed together. Her shaking eased.

'You know, I never used to talk so much, before Terry died.' She sighed. 'It's like I need to get all the words out.'

'Yeah. I understand.' And he did, and he felt like a shit for being so mean. But who was he kidding? He was like that sometimes. His mind jumped back to a night at the pub, right after Aden moved in. Joseph had yelled at an old man for spilling beer down his new white shirt. He could still picture the old guy's face, crumpling at the blast. When the man lurched away, Aden had touched Joseph's hand. 'Joey? Don't be a fuckwit, okay?'

And he'd tried; every year he was better. But Aden was gone now, and he was no good without him.

'It's gonna snow.' Kimmy was calm and resigned.

Joseph glanced back. She'd wrapped her arms around her uninjured leg, drawing it close to her chest.

'We don't get much snow in Lubbock, but I know a snowy sky.'

The clouds pressed closer, blotting out the daylight. The mountain loomed darker. It really did look like snow.

Joseph zipped the windcheater to his chin. The whole trip had been a disaster. The worst thing was, he knew it was because of him. If Aden was here, they'd be friends with half the hotel guests and Aden would be thrilled by summer snow. Joseph had a flash of their ski holiday years ago in New Zealand – Aden grinning, sticking his tongue out to catch snowflakes as they rode the lift, poles balanced on their laps. The clamp around Joseph's throat grew vice-like and he coughed to release it.

Then he was crying, at first a silent shaking, and though he tried to stop, he gasped and wept.

'Joe?' Kimmy turned.

He felt her palm on his back, the small, kind heat of it.

The first cold flake landed on his cheek.

'Never mind. Never mind.' Kimmy rubbed his back as the snow fell faster. 'Whatever it is, you'll be okay.'

He wanted so much to believe her.

The voices of Birta and the others were closer. He wiped his face with his scarf.

Snow swirled down, blew across the ice, gathered softly on the laces of his boots.

THE LESSON

S TACEY WROTE NEATLY ON THE whiteboard, never fully turning her back. She was young but she wasn't stupid.

'Miss. Miss! Demetri farted!' Lawson staggered to his feet, clutching his neck. 'Help! I can't breathe!'

'Sit down please, Lawson.' Stacey heard her plaintive tone and knew she'd be ignored. She'd watched the other teacher with the seniors, and for all his laid-back, barely there approach he had an underlying steel. When Brian wanted obedience, his voice flattened and his eyes turned cold. She'd tried the same expression without response. She suspected she looked like she was squinting at the class.

'But Miss, it stinks!' Lawson careered into a wall lined with charcoal self-portraits and his friends laughed, drumming on the desks. The din rose in the room and a pulse began in Stacey's temple. The guard on the verandah shot her a look through the bank of windows, and she smiled back, trying for serene. Jeff had been helpful, but she had to start managing herself.

'Lawson, that's enough!'

The boy pulled his shirt over his mouth, sucking air in and

out with an exaggerated wheeze. 'He's gassing us! Evacuate, evacuate!'

Demetri scowled, holding his desk like a flotation device. The boy hadn't gelled with the others; somehow in his thirteen years he hadn't learnt to fake a laugh, hadn't figured out how to roll with the punches. His classmates hounded and harassed him. Only Tom showed the surly, skinny boy any kindness.

Tom sat attentive in his back-row desk. The rest of the class hooted and yelled and stamped their feet. Stacey stood with hands on hips. There was no point competing with the noise, but she hoped the boys would settle. Tom picked up a pen and began writing.

The classroom door swung open and a grey-haired woman in a pantsuit stood in the doorway.

'Good morning, Juniors.'

'Good mor-ning, Mizz Leiii-chardt.' They chanted the greeting in the slow, slurred way that made Stacey shiver. She didn't know why each student was here – she'd asked not to be told – but she knew juvenile detention was for kids gone far astray. Serial thieves, repeat arsonists. Violent offenders.

'Young Lawson, having trouble staying put?' The principal glared at the stocky youth. 'Perhaps you need a job? The groundsman would love your help.' She turned. 'Let's go.'

Lawson shuffled out behind her, still smoothing down his shirt.

Stacey stepped back to the whiteboard, ears burning. She pointed to the story arc, with its brightly coloured arrows. 'So, you've seen how a story works. Time to get writing.'

~

Stacey leant on the weathered grey fence post. The sun gave one last wink and dropped out of sight, outlining the trees on the hill in gold. Cockatoos screeched above her, winging their way across dry brown paddocks, heading for the river. She lifted her phone and pressed the button.

With a few quick edits, the overgrazed station looked idyllic – the sky now royal blue morphing to flame-orange at the horizon. Stacey added a caption: *Booralla beauty #blessed.* Filter or no filter, the land here had a strange appeal, with its rocky outcrops and strong, sharp light. On this rise in the road, there were two bars of reception. She posted the picture.

Zipping the mobile into her running belt, she jogged towards town. Every day she ran like this, trying to throw off her loneliness. Sometimes for a whole evening she was content – reading or planning lessons with a glass of wine. Sometimes she outran her tears only to find them again in the kitchen of the rented flat.

She'd been happy at the start. Or excited, at least, by the challenge. None of her Sydney friends would have considered working here. She was proud, telling people about her job. It wasn't her dream position but she was grateful to have work; not all new graduates were so lucky. And the boys, these damaged boys – they were just kids, after all. They needed patience and understanding.

But it was quiet. There was nothing to do, nowhere to go except the shops, the pubs and a greasy-floored McDonald's. The locals were kind, inviting her to barbecues, but she resisted. She didn't want their pity, and she was bored by talk of rainfall and livestock.

Three months into the posting, her students were unchanged. They pushed her every day, poking and prodding. Tom was easygoing, but he'd arrived like that. The rest of them made up for it, testing her limits in small, relentless ways.

Her energy was fading, draining out into the red Booralla dust.

~

'Wow, Tom. Fantastic work.' *This* made it all worthwhile. His story was good. Simple, honest, pared back. 'You really nailed it!' She knew she was gushing but she couldn't seem to stop.

They were sitting at a round table down the back of the classroom. It was lunchtime, and the other students were outside, kicking a battered football between buildings as guards surveyed them from the shade.

Tom fiddled with the hem of his shirt. He was so small, more like eleven than fourteen. His caseworker had once mentioned Tom's mother had been on and off heroin for much of his childhood. Stacey guessed there hadn't always been enough food.

She smoothed the stapled paper in front of her. 'I'd like to put this in a writing competition.'

Tom frowned. 'Yeah, nah. Don't think so.'

'Why not?' she asked. 'What have you got to lose?'

He looked at her and in that instant she saw the betrayals he'd endured. Of course he was wary.

Stacey pushed down her emotions, staring out to the concrete cell blocks. She'd give him space, allow him time to speak.

'They'd just laugh. I can't write all fancy.' Tom's cheeks were flushed beneath his freckles. She had an urge to stroke his downy skin.

'They wouldn't, no way. Your story's really good. It's clear, it's real …' Stacey stopped. Tom was twisting in his seat.

She changed tack. 'Just let me enter it, hey? The winner gets two hundred dollars. A hundred for second.'

Tom's head snapped up. 'You serious?'

'As a heart attack.'

His eyebrows raised a fraction. They grinned at each other.

Tom scratched his neck, gazing out at his classmates playing kick-to-kick. He turned to Stacey. 'Okay. Okay, you can send it. Just don't tell the other guys.'

~

The sun was already hot on Stacey's head as she hurried from the car park. She'd been away sick the past two days, and she felt oddly light, as if her bones were too thin. She made it to the covered area just as the students filed across from the cell blocks. The boys sat on rows of bench seats, talking and jostling until the principal stepped up to the microphone.

'Gentlemen, we have a star in our midst.' Jill Leichardt beamed at Stacey's junior class in the front two rows.

Stacey's stomach fluttered, and suddenly she knew.

Ms Leichardt's shiny red lips stretched and contracted around her words. 'One of our clever year eight boys has come second in a high school writing competition – the Write Here Write Now award. Tom, can you step forward?'

For a moment it seemed he wouldn't, but at last he emerged from the group and slumped to the front. The dozen other junior boys were unusually attentive – quiet on the benches, facing the front.

'Tom receives a certificate and a hundred dollars. We'll keep the cheque safe for you, Tom.'

Ms Leichardt shook his hand, smiling her terrifying grin. Tom grasped her hand swiftly. He edged back to his seat as the principal leant close to the microphone, which squealed in protest. The assembled boys snickered, but Ms Leichardt waited until the feedback died away.

'We're so very proud of you, Tom.'

There was a beat of silence, then someone called out in a mincing voice, 'So proud of you, *Tom-Tom!*'

A chill ran along Stacey's spine, like the downdraft before a storm. But she was thrilled for Tom. He'd understand once she explained. Deep down he must be happy too.

She surveyed the seated boys, her gaze falling on Tom's tousled sandy head, bent over his certificate. Her eyes watered. Finally she'd made a difference here.

As Stacey led the class back to the demountable, she gave Tom a quick thumbs up. He ducked his chin, and she wasn't sure he'd seen. A few boys teased and shoved him, but Stacey didn't intervene – these days she chose her battles.

In the classroom, the boys returned to their experiment – making sugar crystals in long, icy strings. Last lesson, the science project had caught their attention. Tom and his friends had even let Demetri join them. But today was different. Demetri was on his own. The other boys made crude remarks and walked about for no reason, and she had to keep steering them back on task.

She was at her desk marking homework when Tom appeared.

'Tom. You gave me a fright.'

He held a piece of sugar-crusted string aloft, his eyes bright and his head raised high. His win had given him new confidence. She swelled to think how she'd inspired him to success.

'Can we use the measuring tape? To see whose crystals are the longest?'

'Sure ...' Like Brian, she kept a single soft measuring tape for use under supervision. She rustled in her drawer, found the coil of tape and handed it across. 'And Tom, about the competition ...' But the boy had turned and in a few strides he was bent over his desk.

Stacey sighed and resumed her marking.

A few minutes later, he was beside her once more.

'Can I have a cloth, Miss?'

She peered at his small, earnest face. 'What for?'

'We spilt water in the storeroom.'

She glanced to the back, where Dan and Arlo hovered in the storeroom doorway. 'Sure. There are rags just there.' She pointed to a box on the shelving near her desk. Tom grabbed a cloth and returned to his friends.

Stacey ticked with her red pen, and made the odd comment in the margin: *Keep up the good work. Punctuation, please.*

Outside, the groundsman whirred across the play area on a ride-on mower and the smell of cut grass wafted through open louvres. Stacey's eyes drifted to her phone. She picked it up, clicked on Instagram. Sixty-three likes for her windmill shot.

There was a clang of metal, and a muffled thud from down the back. Three boys emerged from the storeroom.

'Tom, Arlo, Dan. What's going on?'

'Nothing. Just cleaning up.' Tom's voice was higher than normal. He smirked and his friends muttered as they strolled to their desks.

Stacey stood, scanning the desktops. They were covered in spilled sugar, string and paperclips. 'You need to sort out those desks.'

'We're on it, Stacey.' Tom's face was gleeful, and his friends chuckled.

For a moment, she was unable to reply.

She stood taller. 'That's Ms Barber to you.'

'Yes, Miss Barber-to-you.'

The class erupted in raucous laughter, and Lawson tipped his chair until he fell off, rolling about on the floor.

'That's e-nough!' Tears pushed at the back of her eyes. She had to gain control – of the class and of herself. 'Lawson, clean the whiteboard. The rest of you – put the science gear away.'

The boys chatted and joked as they ambled to and fro across the room.

'Hurry up. I'm going to count down from ten and anyone still standing when I'm done can see Ms Leichardt. Ten, nine, eight …'

The movement became faster and there was less talk.

'Seven, six, five, four …'

Most of the boys were in their seats now.

'Three, two, *one.*'

Demetri wasn't in his seat. The room seemed to tilt. Had he absconded? But Jeff was on the verandah, right near the door.

'Where's Demetri?' She flung her chair back, sending it rolling into the wall.

The boys became busy, rummaging in their books. A few glanced at Tom.

'I said, where's Demetri?' Her legs were weak. 'Tom?'

'Dunno.'

She strode between chairs – hot, angry steps. She was almost at Tom's desk when she spotted Demetri.

The dark-haired boy lay on the storeroom floor, limp and still. His hands were tied behind him with the measuring tape, and his ankles were bound with a shoelace. His mouth was stuffed with rag, pulled tightly around his head. His eyes were closed and mucus streamed from his nose.

'Oh my God.' Stacey rushed to his side, her fingers working at the knot behind his head, then tugging and yanking fabric from the boy's mouth. His chest still rose and fell, but his face was powder white. She ripped the tape measure from his wrists and brought his arms in front, bending one knee to place him in recovery position.

'Bring me the phone,' she called.

Boys hovered in the doorway, gaping. Tom blinked and stared. No one moved. The boys breathed loudly, shoulders heaving, seeming to breathe in unison.

Her fear and outrage boiled together. 'Bring me the phone, you fucking *animals!*'

Tom's eyes widened.

Jeff burst in from the verandah. 'What's going on?' His bulk filled the storeroom entrance. 'Geez …'

'Call an ambulance. I think he's unconscious.'

Stacey rubbed the boy's arm. 'Wake up, Demetri. Come on.' She watched him and willed him to open his eyes.

~

Stacey leant on her desk, unable to stop shaking. Out on the verandah, the boys were pumped up, talking over each other. Jeff and a support guard moved down the line, checking for contraband. The class would return to their cell blocks as soon as they'd been cleared. Tom, Dan and Arlo would go straight to isolation.

Stacey unlocked the top drawer of the filing cabinet. A muscle twinged in her shoulder as she hoisted her handbag onto the desk.

She fumbled for her keys. She'd wait until the class was gone, then drive to her flat to pack. She couldn't face them, those vicious boys. Even Tom. Especially Tom.

She caught a flicker of movement as the class began to file away. Tom, second-last in line, stood close to the window, the freckles stark on his narrow face. He opened his mouth as if he might speak and his arm flew up, fingers stretched towards her. He gazed through the glass, raw and forlorn.

Her heart cracked open and she lifted a hand. But even as she watched, the boy's expression changed, hardened. He rotated his wrist and showed his middle finger.

Water pooled into her eyes and Tom's image rippled and blurred.

She kept her hand raised as the line moved off, waving like a fool until all the boys were gone.

THE
FLUTTERING

'Let's go fast. Use your legs, go, go!' Liam pushed harder on the tricycle handle as his son's chubby knees rose and fell. He liked to take Thad outside after he brought him home from day care. It was good for them both – time together, fresh air. But also, he liked to tire his son out so he'd give Liam a couple of hours' peace after dinner.

'Bery fast!' Thad grinned back at Liam.

'You sure are.'

The street was quiet and the air had an edge of chill. It was late May and the sun was sliding down the far slopes of Mount Coot-tha. Fruit bats flapped high above them, heading for backyard gardens and flowering trees.

'Almost home now. Time for dinner.'

They trundled along the footpath.

'Sausages?'

'No, mate, my famous pasta bake.' Liam raised his hand to greet an old lady watering flowers behind a peeling fence, glancing away from her eager eyes.

'Yuck. Doan like it.'

'Well, that's what we're having.'

They continued at a gentle roll, stopping across from their house. Liam always felt a leap of hope as they arrived, as if Jess might appear and say, 'Hello, my boys!' But the front door stayed closed, the verandah dark in the shadow of the gum tree in the corner of the yard.

'Birdy.' Thad pointed upwards.

'What?' Liam craned to see. The tree had started losing leaves and the remaining growth looked sickly pale. It had been struck by lightning in the huge storm the day before the funeral. He kept meaning to call someone, have it removed.

'Up dere. Birdy for me.'

Liam squinted through the foliage. As he tried to spot the bird, a wide-winged shape flew honking from the sky, landing on a branch.

'Two birdies for me.' Thad gazed up, his cheeks flushed.

'Sure, they can be your birds.' Liam hoped the ibises weren't planning to stay. A flock had nested there for months last year, disturbing Jess with their jarring calls. They'd left with the storm, disappearing overnight.

Thad released the handlebars and stood, beaming, reaching for the birds. His chubby hands opened and closed.

Liam helped Thad off the tricycle. 'Let's cross the road, hey?' He steered the trike as they walked towards the house. The evening light was fading. A cold breeze rustled down the street.

At the front gate, Thad dragged. 'Birdies.' His eyes were round and bright, his lips rosy red.

Liam shivered. 'Yeah, birdies, now let's get some dinner.' He wheeled the tricycle under the steps and held his son's hand as they trudged upstairs.

~

Liam clicked the night-light on, then switched off the bedroom light. 'There we go.'

He sat on the bed and leant to kiss Thad. His son's forehead was warmer than usual, but he seemed fine. He'd played in the bath and eaten a fair amount of dinner, considering it was tuna bake.

'Night, matey.'

'Night, Daddy.'

Liam hovered in the doorway as his son drew himself into a bundle, legs folded under his tummy, his green soft toy Dino tucked under one arm. Thad had asked about his mum every day for a week, then stopped, like a tap being turned off. Since then, he'd moved from nappies to undies, and changed from cot to bed without a drama.

In the kitchen, Liam stacked the dishwasher and washed the pots and lunchboxes. Once or twice he thought he heard an ibis – that hollow, harsh cry – but when he paused, hands in the soapy water, the only sound was the faint droning music from the teenager next door.

He wiped the bench and pressed 'start' on the dishwasher, then turned the kitchen light off. He locked the front door, then the back door. All the jobs Jess used to do. He'd been the cook, and always first into bed. Now he was everything.

In the bedroom he changed into boxers and sat propped on pillows. He wasn't tired yet but he craved the comfort of the rumpled queen bed. If he lowered his face to the doona, he could still smell Jess, her scent barely there.

Liam picked up his iPad, checked emails. So many messages from friends and family, some three or four months old. The longer he left them, the worse he felt, but he could never work out how to reply. *I'm wrecked. I want her back.* People didn't need that.

He checked her emails too. The messages flooded in – nursing union bulletins, Witchery and Dotti ads, requests for donations from The Wilderness Foundation, all addressed *Dear Jessica*, as if she was still alive. And a new email from her sister. These were the worst – unbearable to read. Lately he just deleted them.

He shut down mail, opened Safari. His pulse pushing up a notch, he typed in *ibis*.

For the next half-hour, Liam jumped from site to site. He flicked through silly videos that failed to make him laugh. He read about ibises on Wikipedia. Then he found an article on ancient Egypt. It said ibises were bred, then sacrificed, to accompany pharaohs to the afterlife – placed in clay urns or in bird-shaped wooden containers and buried in tombs. X-rays of the buried birds showed all their necks were broken. Liam enlarged the pictures of the narrow necks bent double. Unease settled in his stomach and he closed the laptop.

Dragging the doona to his chin, Liam turned towards the wall, ibises and broken bones revolving in his mind. A possum stomped across the roof. Thad called out – a single, garbled word. Finally, a silence descended on the house and Liam began to drift.

~

The alarm blared beside the bed and Liam sat bolt upright. Thad never slept this long. Each morning he appeared in Liam's bedroom just after five.

Liam hurried to his son's room.

Thad was awake, lying on his back, examining the fingers of one hand.

Liam's shoulders sagged with relief. 'Good morning! You feeling lazy today, huh?'

Thad waved. 'Hi, Daddy.'

'Thinking of getting up anytime soon?' Liam scooped his son up, doona and all, and carried him out to the kitchen.

'Here you go.' He deposited Thad in his booster-seat. 'Weet-Bix or toast?'

Thad's eyes were glassy. 'No tank you, Daddy.' He wormed down from the chair, wandering through the living room.

Even from the kitchen, Liam could hear the piping voice. 'Birdies? Birdies for me.' He remembered his strange anxiety the night before.

Glancing at the clock, he sighed. It was already quarter past six and they'd be late if he didn't get them both fed and dressed and out the door. He strode to the front verandah and found Thad on the top step, angling his head to stare up into the leaves.

'Come on, mate. Come have your breakfast.'

Thad gaped, his fingers stretched towards the birds.

Liam took his son's hand to pull him back inside, but Thad resisted, beginning to cry. Liam knelt to feel Thad's hot, dry forehead, and his heart skipped a beat. Any illness terrified him now.

'Come on, little man.' He carried his son to the sofa and flicked on a cartoon. He'd phone the doctor's surgery as soon as it opened.

~

The appointment wasn't until late afternoon and the doctor was running behind, but at least she was thorough, checking Thad's ears, throat, chest and stomach. Thad sat on Liam's lap, then lay on the examination table without moving. He was pale and hardly spoke.

'Well, he's definitely warm but there's nothing else to find. He's hydrated and alert, the urine test was clear. It's most likely a virus.'

Liam nodded. 'He's been alright at home – just watching TV and drinking lemonade.' He paused. 'I hope that's okay. My wife used to give him lemonade if he was sick.'

The doctor tapped away at her keyboard. 'Lemonade's fine, if that gets him drinking. Water's good too. Keep up the Panadol. If he gets worse, bring him back.'

'Thanks, doc.' Liam lifted Thad.

As they drove home, Thad was silent. The sun was low and cars passed with their lights on. Liam carried Thad from the ute and started up the steps.

'Daddy! More birdies!'

Liam gripped his son's small body. Half-a-dozen ibises perched high in the tree.

'Yeah. Birdies.' He'd begun to hate them, with their long, cruel beaks, their leathery black heads. He imagined them simmering with anger, their narrow necks aching in remembrance.

The birds crouched together on the branch, outlined against the twilight.

'Birdies come for me.' Thad placed his palms together.

Liam drew the boy's head close. 'How about a bath?' He continued up the steps and inside.

Thad's teeth chattered as Liam helped him undress. When he climbed into the bath, he cried out that the water was burning his feet. Panicked, Liam snatched him up and checked the temperature, but it was only warm.

'It's because you're sick, that's all. Let's try again.' Shirt plastered wet to his chest, he lowered Thad back in, feet clear of the water. His son looked worried, then relaxed, letting Liam support him until his feet dangled free in the water.

'Nice, Daddy.'

Liam closed his eyes for half a second. It was going to be okay. He could manage a childhood illness. Other parents did it all the time.

He bundled Thad into PJs and convinced him to eat a few crackers. Settling him in bed, Liam smoothed the boy's hair. He was cooler.

Liam switched on the night-light. 'Sweet dreams, little man.'

~

Liam woke to darkness and a feeling of dread. He'd been dreaming of giant ibises, hooting and flapping towards him.

He realised Thad was whimpering from his room. 'Daddy. Daddy.'

Liam staggered up.

Thad lay curled on his side. On the sheet near his head was a puddle of half-digested crackers. He frowned at Liam. 'I did a bomit.'

'It's okay. Daddy will fix it.'

Liam began to lift his son, but Thad cried out and Liam eased him back onto the mattress.

'What? What hurts?'

'Don't know.' Thad began to wail, and Liam wiped his son's cheeks, the tears smearing across a blazing heat.

He sat on the bed, his mind racing. Jess would have known what to do. She was always so sensible, but she'd believed in trusting your instincts too. Liam was getting a powerful bad feeling.

'I'm just going to make a phone call, buddy. I'll be right back.'

When he returned, he crouched beside Thad. 'We're going to go in an ambulance soon. They'll make you better, at the hospital.'

Thad murmured something, his lips dry and flaking.

Liam leant closer. 'What's that?'

His son whispered, 'Da birdies. Da birdies want me.' His focus flicked from one point to another in the room, as if searching among the stuffed toys, the 'Thad' cross-stitch on the wall, the family photo on the dresser.

Liam patted Thad's leg. 'No they don't. They don't.' He took deep breaths as he waited for the ambulance. 'They're just birds.'

~

'The good news is, all the tests are normal.' Dr Joosten's gaze strayed towards the corridor. The children's intensive care unit was busy, staff bustling from one room to the next. 'I'll just be a minute,' the doctor said, raising an arm to a nurse lingering outside the glass panel. His shirt was damp at the armpit.

The light tube in the ceiling above Thad's bed was buzzing, and Liam had an intense urge to rip it out.

'Sorry,' Dr Joosten said. His eyes were bloodshot and had deep lines around the edges. 'Now, like I was saying, all the tests so far have come back clear. No signs of infection in his bloodwork, no inflammation. And he's no worse today. However ...' His gaze shifted onto Thad, who lay like a shadow beneath the sheets. 'He's obviously not well.' Thad was chalky white, slipping from alertness to sleep then back again.

'No,' Liam said, more loudly than he intended. He folded his arms. 'So, what's the next step?'

A flicker passed across Dr Joosten's face, and Liam realised the man had no idea.

'Well, we're monitoring him very closely, of course. And the next twenty-four hours should provide some clarity as to the nature of his diagnosis.'

Liam bowed his head. He might be a foreman not a doctor, but he knew a bunch of bullshit when he heard it. 'Right.'

'Excuse me, I have to get going.' Dr Joosten began to walk away. 'Let the nurses know if you have any concerns.'

Liam moved next to Thad. 'Hi there.'

'Hi, Daddy.'

'The doctor says you're going to be okay.' He felt a tingling in his scalp, like at Christmas, when he'd talked about Santa. He'd never liked lying, but sometimes with kids you felt you had to. It seemed to be what people did.

'We go home now? See da birdies?'

The buzzing of the light above grew louder. Those fucking birds.

He forced himself to speak calmly. 'Sure, mate. When you're better.' He rubbed his face, stubble grazing his fingers.

Thad's nurse, Tenielle, paused at the door. 'Have you been home yet? Since he first came in?'

Liam shook his head. 'I don't want to leave him. He's so croo—' He broke off, aware of Thad's attention. 'My sister's coming from Melbourne tomorrow. I'll go home for a bit then.'

Tenielle stood beside the bed. 'I understand how you feel. But he knows me now, right?' She made a thumbs-up sign and

Thad copied her, his thumb raised just above the sheet. 'Why don't you take a break?'

Liam felt a fraction better. In a big hospital like this, they'd figure out the problem.

'Okay. I might just have a shower and shave, change my clothes.'

Tenielle pulled the bedsheet up to Thad's shoulders. 'Great idea. I'll keep a close eye on him.'

Liam bent over Thad. 'See you very soon.' He knew the perfect thing to say. 'I'll bring Dino back.'

'Yes!' Thad raised his head. 'Bring Dino.'

Liam waved and left while his son was happy, driving home in the pink evening light.

He parked the ute and sat for a moment, weariness settling in his limbs. A couple walked by with their dog and he watched them, amazed at their carefree faces. He cracked the door and put a foot onto the bitumen.

Jess spoke to him, soft and soothing. *Just get sorted, go back to Thaddeus.*

She always called their son Thaddeus – the awkward, odd name she'd chosen, one he'd agreed to without a word of complaint because Jess was already sick, just diagnosed.

'Yeah, okay.' He got out and slammed the door.

In the open air, there was a fluttering sound. He steeled himself to look.

A huge flock of ibises shuffled and shifted high in the gum tree, their curved beaks silhouetted. There were too many to count – a hundred or more. A musty stink filtered down from the tree. On a low branch, an ibis stretched its wings, the slash of scarlet showing underneath.

Liam's hands became fists, sudden knowledge sweeping through him.

He ran onto the footpath, yelling, but the birds didn't move. He grabbed a rock from the garden edge and threw it, but it bounced off the trunk, falling harmlessly to the grass.

'You could try a pressure hose.'

He jumped at the voice. The teenager next door, the one who played that shitty music, was washing a car in the driveway. His spotty face was perplexed.

Liam turned another rock over in his hand. 'Yeah.' He felt embarrassed, his revelation less certain. 'Think I'll leave them alone.' Thad was waiting for him, maybe starting to get upset.

He ran up the front steps. Inside, he showered and dressed in fresh clothes, grabbed Dino and hurried back to the hospital.

~

Outside Thad's room, Liam stopped dead. Several figures clustered about his son's bed. A trolley sat near the drip stand. Discarded packets lay scattered on the floor.

'Are you the father?' It was a male nurse he'd never seen before, coming down the hallway.

Liam stared at him. 'I'm his dad, yes. I'm his dad.'

'We need to keep back, so the doctors can help him.' The nurse spoke slowly and clearly.

'Fuck.' Liam strode to the end of the bed. 'What's going on?'

Thad's eyes were closed. There was an oxygen mask on his face. A monitor bleeped a steady rhythm.

The doctors glanced at Liam then resumed their work, one watching the monitors, the other injecting something into the drip in Thad's arm. Tenielle was holding a tiny glass container, sucking the contents up into a syringe.

Liam could taste silty toothpaste. He squeezed Thad's dinosaur.

The male nurse stood beside Liam. 'He's stable now. We don't know what happened but he's okay. I'll explain things if you come with—'

Liam reached for his son's foot beneath the blankets. 'You'll be right, mate,' he said, his voice strangled. The surge of instinct was stronger than ever. He had to stop the birds.

Jess whispered in his ear, low and urgent. *Yes, go. Go now.*

Liam placed Dino on the bed. 'I won't be long.'

The nurse's eyebrows rose, and his mouth opened, but Liam bolted before the man could speak.

~

At first the axe just bounced off the trunk. Liam let out a yell, the sound echoing down the dark street like a taunt. He gathered his fury and unleashed a massive strike, jolting the big tree and sending birds screeching into the air. The axe wedged in the wood and Liam yanked it out, then hacked again.

'Go!' he yelled as the birds wheeled around, their bodies ghostly in the night. *'Go!'*

He attacked the trunk, swinging wildly, but each blow landed in a different place. The bark began to ooze where he'd gashed it. This was ridiculous; it would take hours. God knew what the tree would hit coming down. And the ibises had returned.

'Fuuuuuck! Just go!' Liam gave the tree one last hit and stood panting. The streetlights blinked on, up and down the road. High above, the birds' eyes glinted as they moaned and crooned.

Panic rose within him and he couldn't think, could hardly breathe. He was going to lose his son too.

'Um, are you okay?'

The teenager next door stepped out of the shadows, the glow of a cigarette in his hand.

'Does it look like I'm okay?'

The kid flinched, and Liam wished his words back.

'Sorry. I'm not okay. My son, Thaddeus—' He stopped, his throat thick. *Thaddeus, courageous heart.*

Liam took a breath, tried again. 'He's really crook, in hospital. They don't know what's wrong.'

The kid nodded.

The foul odour filled Liam's nostrils. He lifted his eyes to the flock in the tree. 'I need to get rid of those fucking birds.'

The kid peered up into the darkness. 'Yeah, they're disgusting. They keep crapping on the cars.' He tapped ash from the cigarette.

Something clicked in Liam's brain.

'You got a lighter?'

The kid frowned. 'What for?' He pulled a plastic cylinder from his pocket and tossed it over.

Liam ran under the house, returning with a jerry can. The kid stepped on his smoke.

Liam splashed the grey gum with petrol, sloshing as high as his head. He thought of the dying dry leaves and felt hope flowing back. He flicked the lighter at the base of the tree.

Flames danced up the bark, all around. Orange and yellow tongues licked the trunk as Liam and the kid watched. The scent of burning eucalypt drifted across, pungent and fresh. Smoke streamed like a signal to the night sky. When the fire reached the lowest branches, the birds began to shriek, rising up in a clamour, their angry cries circling the house.

'Leave my son alone!' Liam screamed. He was shaking. The tree burned bright now – a pyre, a triumph.

The birds flew around the house – once, twice, three times – then away to the west. Their furious calls receded, until the only sound was the crackling of leaves.

Liam could see neighbours on their landings and at their front doors, framed by light. A distant siren grew louder, but the tree was almost destroyed.

'I'll stay. You go.' The kid pointed to his pressure hose, coiled on the grass. 'I can handle it.' He had a steadiness that made Liam want to weep.

Liam ran a hand across his face. 'Thank you. Thanks.' He sprinted to the ute and pulled away.

~

The unit was hushed, just the muted blip of heartbeats from each room. The smell of lemon floor cleaner hung in the air. Behind the central desk, a doctor wrote in a chart. Thad's bed was empty, the sheet crumpled and Dino abandoned. Liam clutched the end of the bed, his legs weak.

'You're back.' Tenielle stood in the doorway. Her face was tired.

Liam searched her features for sympathy, that awful, dripping look people gave you when you lost someone, but there was nothing like that.

'He's on the loo. Thad, I mean. He insisted on getting up. Someone else is with him.' She moved to the bedside, her expression perplexed. 'No one can believe it. How quickly he's recovered.'

Liam's eyes stung and he blinked in the subdued light. 'So he's okay? He's getting better?'

Tenielle smiled. 'It's the most incredible thing. We were trying everything but he was still unresponsive.' She straightened the sheets as she spoke. 'Then suddenly, he sat up. He said, "Bye, birdies." And he was fine.'

'Shit.' Liam stared at the vacant bed, the hairs on his arms rising up.

'I know. He seems completely well. No fever, normal obs. It's crazy, right?'

Liam lifted Dino from the blankets. 'It's crazy alright.'

Tenielle walked to the door. 'He won't be long.'

'Thanks.' Liam lowered himself into a plastic chair by the bed. He held the dinosaur in trembling hands.

Good work, babe. Jess sounded so happy and proud.

A moment later, Thad's sweet voice echoed down the hall.

~

'One more story?'

'No, mate, it's seven-thirty. You need sleep.' Liam slotted books into the bookcase.

'Oh, Dad-dyyyy.' Thad was getting to that whiny, overtired stage. He seemed well since his hospital stay last month, but he was exhausted by bedtime, a reminder of his ordeal.

Liam sat beside his son and reached for his hands. One was closed around something ruffled.

He stiffened. 'Show Daddy.'

Thad unrolled his fingers. On his palm lay a black-and-white feather, folded in half. The markings were distinct.

'Where did you get that?' Liam asked.

Thad swished the broken feather through the air. 'Whee, whee, fly birdy.'

Liam rushed to the window and threw it open. The only sounds were bleats of music from next door. Outside his son's bedroom, the blackened tree stood like a warning. The tree loppers were coming the next day.

'Thad, give it to Daddy.' He held out his hand.

Thad tucked his fist beneath his arm. 'My fedder.'

Liam clenched his teeth. He wanted to prise the feather from his son's stubborn grip, burn it to ash. But he was being irrational. Thad was fine. The birds were gone. It was an old feather from the yard.

Liam forced himself to smile. 'Give it to Daddy, then we can have one more story.'

Thad hesitated, his mouth uncertain. He offered up the damp, bedraggled item.

Liam lifted it between finger and thumb, holding it at arm's length.

'You choose a book, okay?' He walked to the door. When he turned, his son was watching.

Liam shook his head. 'Sorry, mate, I have to take it. You could get sick again.'

In the kitchen, he shoved the feather to the bottom of the bin. As he returned, Thad was climbing onto the bed with *Wombat Stew.*

Liam sprawled beside his son. His muscles were finally beginning to relax. Soon he would tunnel into his own bed and let sleep overtake him. Maybe he would dream of Jess. Maybe he'd dream of something new, like the camping trip he planned to take with Thad.

Thad opened the book, and cried out with joy. 'Look, Daddy!'

A black-and-white feather lay between them on the bed.

THE GROUND BENEATH

ON SUNDAY SHE WENT TO mow and there it was – a round, damp hole the size of a rubbish bin. It sat like a pockmark in the centre of the lawn. She stood beside the lawnmower, tugging her shirt down. She wasn't surprised, though she knew she should be. It seemed typical of her life. The toaster was burning bread on the lowest setting, the kettle had started leaking and the car was making a clunking sound.

On Monday she phoned the council. She waited on hold, smiling at other teachers in the staffroom, shrugging sheepishly at those who passed her more than once. Her ear was going numb. The minutes ticked by, as a message cooed at intervals, 'Thank you for calling Greater Bendigo City Council. We'll be with you shortly.' She scratched at a mark on her nylon pants. It looked like chocolate.

At last a voice chirped down the line, 'Water and sewerage, you're speaking with Jason!'

'Oh hello, this is Veena Lal. I have a problem in my backyard.'

'Does this relate to water and sewerage?' Jason had already lost his bounce.

'Yes, I think so. I'd say so.' How could she know? It drove her crazy, all this classification, this pigeonholing. Like her GP – sending her to the neurologist, then the gastroenterologist, and another specialist tomorrow. It seemed like everyone was just passing the buck.

'Perhaps you could tell me the nature of your problem?' The man's tone was brisk now.

'Well, there's a bit of a hole in my lawn.'

'There's a hole in your lawn,' he repeated.

'Yes, a *big* hole,' Veena rushed to say. 'Maybe half a metre wide, a metre deep.' There was a silence down the line.

'Ma'am, that sounds like a domestic concern. Perhaps your husband could help? Or a neighbour?'

Veena opened her mouth, then closed it.

'Yes. Okay, thank you.' She put her phone away and wiped the sweat from her top lip.

The room buzzed with teachers talking and eating around her. She sat in the vinyl armchair, making cheerful conversation when others stopped to chat. Her waistband was a vice and her thighs strained the fabric of her pants. She had to stop buying Tim Tams.

~

Each day the hole was bigger. The sight of it made her heart pound. She'd told no one but the man from the council. Rohan wouldn't care – she was no longer his problem. Her sons were overseas – one travelling, one working; they'd only make jokes she'd have to laugh at. Her sisters in Sydney couldn't fix this. And her friends here had their own troubles. So the pit grew – wider, deeper.

Thursday after work, Veena sat near the roses on the worn

wooden bench, a long-ago gift from Rohan. The sun had set, but the day was still light and warm. She twined her hands together in her lap. The sinkhole was as big as a couch. She didn't go near the edge now – frightened by what she'd googled – so she wasn't sure how deep it was. Not too deep, surely. No deeper than a man.

The scent of the pink roses was strong in the air, the sweetness coating the back of her throat. They used to prune the bushes after work, in the lull before dark. She'd been so careful, snipping here and there; he'd been quick and decisive with each cut. They'd loved that time together. At least, she thought they had.

Veena stood up, felt a fluttering behind her breastbone again. She paused, a hand to her neck. She was tired, so tired.

The backyard was in shadow now. She picked across the lawn, keeping to the side, like a mouse skirting a sleeping beast. The hole was as dark as death. She hurried inside and locked the door.

~

In the morning, Veena dragged herself out of bed and along to the kitchen with tight, short steps. Everything seemed to hurt these days.

Lukewarm light filtered through the windows. Her pyjamas were damp around the collar. She slotted a cup under the coffee machine and glanced out to the backyard as the machine growled.

'My God!'

The lawn had disappeared – as if a giant spoon had scooped out all the grass. The rose garden on the left, the veggie patch down the back and the shed in the corner were all intact. But in the oval-shaped centre, where her boys had once played rowdy games of cricket, was a gaping chasm.

She gripped the edge of the sink. She'd left it too long, and now the hole was grotesque. In the pale dawn, it yawned like a mouth. And even as she watched, the bench seat shifted, tipped forward and was swallowed.

Veena stood rooted to the spot. She must act, she knew. But she had an appointment at eight, the very last specialist. The one who might fix everything. Right after the cardiologist, she'd ring. The council again, or a landscaper. Someone who could help.

~

The doctor was young – younger than Veena. She had sleek, auburn hair and friendly blue eyes. Veena smoothed the skirt of her dress as she sat down.

'Well, everything checks out fine. Your pulse, your blood pressure, the ECG. Your stress echo was normal too.'

Veena felt all hope fall away. She would get sicker, and sicker, and die. No one would know why. No one could save her.

Dr Reid was watching. 'Are you okay?'

Veena shook her head, and tears began to fall. She thought of Rohan, her far-flung children, her aching, jumpy heart.

'I have a sinkhole in my yard,' she whispered. She pulled a tissue from her bag and mopped at her face. When she saw the doctor's baffled look, Veena laughed shakily. 'I bet you don't hear that a lot.'

Dr Reid smiled. 'No, I don't, that's for sure. I hope it gets fixed soon.' She paused. 'Veena, if you've just been through a divorce – your GP mentioned it in the letter – that might explain some of your symptoms. Maybe all of them.'

Veena dropped her gaze, toying with the tissue.

Dr Reid continued. 'It's a sort of heartbreak. Your pulse races, you have pains all over, and a terrible fatigue.'

Veena blew her nose. 'So you don't think I'm sick?'

'No. I think you've had a tough time. And being sad can affect you physically.'

'It could be that.' Veena tucked the tissue in her bag. On the hedge outside the window, a willie wagtail swung his tail, hopping and wagging. 'It's probably that,' she acknowledged. She let out a lungful of air.

The doctor spread her freckled hands on the desk. Her ring finger was bare, with a whiter strip of skin. Her voice was soft. 'It happens to a lot of people.'

~

Veena sat on a bench outside the specialist building, squinting across the car park. It was half past eight and the day was as dazzling as Rohan's new teeth.

She wasn't old, not even sixty. She could do so much more. Teach her students with real passion. Join a choir. Hike the El Camino.

She stood and felt her spine uncoil. Her heartbeat paced with her steps – slow and even – as she wound past other vehicles to her car. Driving home, her mind returned to the doctor's words. The more she considered them, the more she sensed their truth.

She swung into her street.

The road was full of cars and trucks. There were firefighters, police and a TV crew. A newsreader stood on the footpath, talking earnestly into a microphone. Neighbours gathered outside their houses, faces aghast, and as Veena rolled towards them, a woman pointed. Veena looked for her house, but couldn't see for all the vehicles parked along the street. Orange hazard cones blocked the way, so she pulled up and climbed out. She stepped from behind a WIN TV truck, and then she saw.

It was gone.

The house was gone. The shed was gone. The gardens were gone. The entire block of land was gone. A vast cavity had consumed it all. The only reminder of her home – the home where she and Rohan had raised their boys – was a familiar red brick, lying loose on the kerb. But she couldn't get to it. The whole area, plus a wide perimeter, was cordoned off.

'Veena.' There was a touch on her arm. Claire, a friend from work, was at her side. 'I saw it on the news. I tried to call but you didn't answer, so I just came.'

Veena's eyes welled up and spilled over. 'Thank you.' She laid her hand over Claire's, and the women walked together to the orange tape.

'That was my house for twenty-eight years.'

Claire shook her head. 'I'm so sorry.' She kept hold of Veena's arm.

A police officer barked into his mobile, 'We need to clear the street. The water guy says there's a cavern down there. Any of these houses could go under.' The neighbours chattered and wandered about. A black labrador dashed from person to person, chased by a frazzled woman calling, 'Toby! *Toby!* Get back here!' The sky above was an opulent blue.

Veena sighed. 'You know what? It's just a house. It's just a bloody house.'

Claire turned quickly, eyebrows raised.

Veena shrugged and lifted her chin. Her cheeks were tight where the tears had already dried.

SWEET
BOUNTIFUL

NIGHTS LIKE THIS, THE SUN setting over the Selkirks, turning the peaks to liquid gold – this is when I see God in our world most clearly. It's like His hand has reached down to touch the earth: *Clara, here I am.* I gaze up from the valley, holding the baby tight to my chest until he wriggles and squirms in his sling. As I head across the lawn with my skirt full of beans, I silently give thanks.

In all the houses around our tiny town, lights are going on and smoke winds up from the chimneys. Swallows wing across the sky, calling to each other. Next door the five Bartley girls trail in from their garden, arms piled with vegetables for their mommas. We smile across the way.

Coming in the screen door, I'm glad to hear Liz in the bathroom, talking over the sound of running water. I lift the blanket on the fort behind the couch, and light spills onto the messy hair of my youngest two.

'Caleb, Joey. Go to Momma Liz, have your bath.'

They race down the hall, always competing.

I tip the beans into a colander and then ease onto the couch, careful not to squish the baby. Bobby's so good; he hardly ever cries. I don't get much time with him, though, because he's Liz's last baby and she says she's trying to drink him in. Bobby was her sixth C-section and the doctor at Cranbrook Hospital told Liz her womb's so thin, another pregnancy would kill her.

'Hey, honey!' Will bangs the back door behind him and comes to sit beside me. The smoky staleness of the city clings to his clothes. Will said I was imagining things when I told him that once, said Cranbrook was only a small city, no pollution to speak of, but my husband smells different in the evenings.

'How was your day?' Will says, but already he's making silly faces at Bobby and soon he holds his arms out to take him.

'Good, and yours?'

'Hel-*lo* there! It's your Dad-dee!'

Bobby is propped on Will's thighs and he starts making happy little gurgles. Will lights up even brighter. 'Clara, did you hear that? He's talking already, only four months old.'

'Oh, he's super smart.'

'I'll take him in to Liz. Get him washed.'

He stands up, holding Bobby against his starched white shirt, still clean and smooth this late in the day. 'I want to get the kids to bed early, so we can talk. You, me and Liz.'

I meet my husband's dark brown eyes. I trust him as I trust God. I should not be fearful.

~

Our children are all asleep, even the eldest, Rachel, who would read a cereal box and has a stack of books beside her bed. Will and Liz sit at one end of the long kitchen table, waiting. I'm scrubbing the second lasagne dish, using more and more detergent.

'Clara.' Our husband speaks firmly but kindly.

I turn, my hands still buried in suds. 'Yes, sorry. I'm coming.' I wipe my hands on my apron, hurry to sit on the other side of Will. Liz and I exchange a glance.

Will reaches out and we each take a hand. His palms are soft since he took the real estate job, but with the sawmill winding down, we're grateful he has work.

'We know plural marriage is our duty,' he says. For once he looks nervous. 'Although I'm happy as we are, a man must have three or more wives to reach the highest realm of heaven.'

Liz and I nod and smile. We've heard this in church, all our lives, yet my smile is stiff, like the collars on Will's new shirts.

'And as your husband, only I can invite you to join me there.'

I chew the side of my tongue to make sure I do not cry. My gaze finds the plaque above the buffet, white with plain black letters: *Keep Sweet*. It is our daily reminder to be even-tempered – never angry, never sad. To keep the Holy Spirit of the Lord within us. I take a deep breath, imagine filling my lungs with goodness and devotion.

'Yes, Will, we know.' Liz draws his hand to her lips. Her hair sparkles under the light, strands of it loose from her bun.

Will straightens, still holding our hands. His eyes shine. 'I'm so proud of you both.' He releases us and smooths his palms on the wood.

We wait. A log shifts in the stove with a thud.

'There's a young woman I think we should court. She's not in Bountiful, she's from Cranbrook. But her family is Fundamental.'

'How old is she?' I ask.

A flicker of a frown crosses Will's face. 'Her name is Beth.'

Shame burns my cheeks, that I didn't ask the name of my future sister wife.

'And she's eighteen.'

I force myself to smile again and Liz speaks for us both. 'I'm sure if you think she's someone special then we will too.'

Will pushes his chair back a little. 'She's young but I think that's important. We can teach her to fit our family. It worked well with you, Clara.'

I think back to when I moved from home, only three streets away, to live with Liz and Will. I'd been seventeen, the eldest of twelve, and excited to finally be assigned. Back then, choosing a husband wasn't permitted, so I was grateful to be matched with a man who wasn't old, a man known to be noble and generous and wise. And I was happy to escape the drudgery of caring for my siblings. Liz was twenty-five, full of energy, with only three children. Joining her and Will in marriage was a dream come true.

Will folds his hands loosely in his lap. 'And of course, Beth can bless us with many more children.'

I look at Liz and her serene expression doesn't falter but I leap in to reply. 'When do we meet her?'

~

It is a bright sunny day, warm for fall. A redtail hawk hovers far above, searching for prey in the fields beyond our yard. The Rocky Mountain maple near the tool shed is changing colour, its leaves blushing orange at the tips. We're at the back of the house, and Will is pointing to a clear space, showing Beth where he plans to extend our home.

Beth is listening, her manner serious. She is tiny, blonde, fragile. I can't imagine her turning a mattress, chopping a pumpkin, lifting a wilful child.

As Will and Beth talk bedrooms and bathrooms, Liz brushes

the back of my hand and I grasp her fingers for a moment. Rachel's reedy voice carries from inside the house, telling Caleb to leave Joey alone. The clothes flap on the line, and I think how they'll be dry by now; I want to fetch the basket and bring them in.

Will and Beth stop talking and turn to us.

'Have you brought the rug?' Will says.

'Yes, it's all ready.' I gesture to the blanket, spread on the fresh-mown grass. The backyard is neat, the garden green from daily watering. Like every yard in Bountiful, it has views of the mountains to both east and west.

'Thank you.' Will walks to the edge of the rug. 'Please join me in prayer.' He stretches a hand to Beth, and I push down a stab of pain. I know this is a test of my faith.

Beth kneels beside Will, and Liz shuffles up beside him too. They link hands. I kneel by Liz. It is the first time I haven't held my husband's hand in family prayer. I close my eyes. A crow calls, loud in the silence.

'Heavenly Father, we pray that you will guide us, and help Beth as she considers joining us here. Help her to feel supported and wanted in our family. Help Liz and Clara to know the true joy that a new sister wife will bring. And help me to steer my family through this period of change, in your infinite wisdom and grace. Amen.' Will's rich baritone resonates between us.

There is quiet then, the wind blowing soft on my cheeks. I feel the Lord's presence, powerful and true. I am filled with love for Will, for Liz, and even for Beth, though I don't yet know her. When Beth joins us, there will be more children, and I will have another close friend, another person I trust above all others. Our family will be stronger.

'Thank you, Lord.' Will stands and as he helps Liz and Beth to their feet he looks across at me and winks. He knows how to do this, how to care for each of us with his affection.

We look towards the Selkirks, grey against the washed-blue sky. I know in my bones we are doing the right thing, bringing Beth into our life. With a sudden rush, I step towards Beth and hug her close. 'We're so glad you're here!' But Beth's arms stay by her side, and when I move away her small face is waxy.

'Well, ladies, let's check the children and have some refreshments, eh?' Will takes Beth's hand. He hasn't noticed her distress, he's grinning at Liz and striding off towards the house. I trail behind, a tangle of worry forming in my stomach.

Inside the house, the children are restless from being cooped-up. Caleb and Joey are playing sword fights with empty Saran Wrap rolls, and Rachel is shouting at them to stop. Abby, Nick and Adam charge off down the long hallway towards the bedrooms. Only little Hannah sits peacefully with crayons, in the centre of the kitchen floor. Liz is at the fridge already, her hip propping the door as she removes the tall jug of iced tea we made this morning.

Will and Beth settle at the table. I slowly unwrap the plate of ginger cookies. Will sends the children away, his voice clipped, but something in Beth's expression is looser than before, and I have an idea.

I place the cookies between my husband and Beth, and touch her shoulder. 'I hope you like these.'

She's so thin, hardly any flesh on her bones, and I think of all the good, strengthening meals we could fix her. The walking she could do, the singing of hymns, the fresh air she could breathe – how healthy she could be, here in Bountiful. How God our heavenly Father could make her whole in our family.

'I'll just be a minute.' I hustle past the bathroom and the boys' bunkroom. Opposite the girls' bunkroom I duck into the nursery, where Hannah has a mattress beside Bobby's wooden cot.

He's snuffling in his sleep, coming to the end of his nap. His round head is warm as I scoop him up, a hand under his bottom and a hand behind his neck, settling him onto my chest. Bobby murmurs but stays asleep, and as I sway down the hall towards the others, I drop my nose to his silky hair. He is sweet and yeasty, like a raisin bun.

When I enter the room, Beth sits hunched, her mouth tight. Will is gesturing and Liz looks concerned.

It takes Beth a second to notice me and Bobby. When she does, her chin lifts. I carry the baby over and kneel at her side. Bobby is waking, turning his head slowly side to side, but as usual he doesn't grizzle, just opens his round blue eyes. I offer him up, and Beth reaches to take him. Will watches, says nothing. I can explain to him later, tell him sometimes I, too, receive guidance from God.

Beth sits the baby in her lap, her knees drawn up to support him. Her eyes sparkle. 'Well hello, little guy! Hello!' Her fair head bends closer, braids dangling. Bobby stares, then reaches with a fat, unsteady hand. Beth laughs, offering him a braid, and he takes it in his chubby baby fist.

'What's his name?' Beth looks at me directly for the first time.

'Robert. But we all just call him Bobby.'

'And he's your youngest?'

I shake my head. All my emotions are in my throat. If I can just explain in the right way, Beth will understand how we live. 'He's *our* youngest. Liz gave birth to him. He's the baby of our family.'

Beth jiggles the baby, beaming as he chews on her hair. I feel sure she understands.

Then Will lays a hand on Bobby's head, right on the place where no bone protects the brain. 'I hope you will bring children into our family too, Beth – as many as the Lord sees fit to give us.'

Straightaway I see this is bad. Beth's face shuts down and she stops moving her knees.

'I want to have a child – children,' she says. 'But I want to study nursing too.'

A ripple of surprise jumps between Liz, Will and me. These days, some Bountiful women work outside the home – in offices and shops in Cranbrook, even as teachers and midwives. But we didn't know about Beth.

'Well, that's okay.' Will is so patient. The light catches the silver hair at his temples and I think again how handsome he is. 'Once you've finished child-bearing, if Liz and Clara agree, you can study part-time. Nursing is a noble pursuit.' He gives Beth a wide smile, and I'm proud. He's trying so hard.

Beth passes Bobby across, her fingers cool as I take the baby. She rubs at a thumbnail, her eyebrows drawn together.

'I want to study soon. Maybe after one or two babies. Maybe now, I don't know.'

I'm so shocked I don't know what to say.

Caleb comes running in. 'Momma, Joey says I'm a slow runner and I'm not, I'm *not!*' He wipes tears from his dirt-smeared cheeks.

'Hush now, Caleb. Go check the henhouse for eggs, eh?' There is sadness in Will's voice, the same disappointment I feel, that Liz must feel too. I push up from beside Beth's chair, holding Bobby close. Caleb's footsteps recede.

Beth stands too. 'I'm sorry. Dad asked me to come, to see for myself, so I said I would.' She lifts her intelligent eyes to mine. 'But I couldn't do this. I could never do this.'

A shiver runs through me. I stare at Liz and Will. They're using pleasant, even tones as they rise from their chairs, telling Beth it's fine, Will can drive her home, it's no trouble at all. They're my loves, my true loves – but things seem off-kilter, like when the piano at church needs tuning.

Beth looks relieved. 'Thank you. May I use the bathroom first?'

I move to show her down the hall. I have an urge to follow her, to ask her questions, but Will puts an arm around me and Bobby, sturdy and encircling. 'First door on the right,' he says.

Beth finds the bathroom and Will keeps holding me. Liz stands beside us, stroking Bobby's cheek. Bobby pushes back from my chest, grinning at Liz, then me, all gums and delight. Slowly the chill in my bones disappears. Everything is fine. All is well.

I remember our bishop's warning – that the Devil plants doubt in our minds.

'She's not a true believer,' I whisper.

'No. She deceived her parents. She misled me too.' Will sighs. 'But we'll continue. We'll find the right person, in time.'

'Someone to join us in true celestial marriage.' Liz wraps her arms around Will and me and Bobby, so close I smell her ginger-cookie breath, feel it on my neck.

Through the huddle I see the wall plaque, and the words that guide our days.

I listen for Beth's footsteps in the hall.

SEA CHANGE

HE PRESSED HIS FINGERTIPS TO his temples, rubbing in small, bleak circles. *What now? What the hell now?* The future played out in his mind – day after day, relentless. Michael tried to breathe deeply but the air in his office was like wool in his lungs. He wedged a finger between his shirt collar and neck, tugging the fabric away from his skin.

His eyes flicked to the painting on the wall opposite his desk. Usually the beach scene with its smooth, untouched sand made his forehead relax. The window to the side revealed only grimy buildings, but the painting held a vision of escape. It was a gift from his ex-wife, and he knew he should get rid of it. Somehow he never had. Today Michael sat staring at the seaside image, his jaw tight. Nothing could help him. No one could. He swore softly as he pushed himself back from the mahogany desk, grabbed his jacket and walked out.

~

The beach was deserted. It was Wednesday, mid-morning, and the dawn surfers and swimmers were long gone. The sky was sapphire, like his daughter's eyes, and cottony clouds huddled at the horizon. The sea rose up in foamy crests that flattened away to turquoise glass. It was more beautiful than he deserved.

Way down the shoreline, Michael could see two mismatched figures linked by outstretched arms – parent and child, he decided. He watched for a moment then stepped off the pavers, his shiny black Windsor Smiths sinking into the sand, fine grains spilling between his socks and the leather.

The sun shone hot on Michael's dark jacket as he stumbled down the path between the dunes, but a breeze off the water lifted his hair and snaked into the gaps between shirt buttons, icy on his skin. He shivered, even as sweat beaded in his armpits.

A seagull squawked as it swooped across, then hovered above him, examining him for signs of food. He raised his arm, shouted, 'Ya!' and the bird veered away. Michael stood squinting in the glare. His legs felt like twigs and his mouth was dry. The smells of fish and salt filled his nostrils, and he wondered if he was elated or destroyed.

Trigg Beach had always been a haven. His parents had brought Michael and his brothers to stay here every summer. He'd learnt to surf – studying the older surfers, emulating them, idolising them. And although he'd gone to university in Perth, when the right time came he'd driven to this beach to propose to Leah. He and Leah and their daughter, Sophie, had taken annual holidays here for sixteen years – until Leah walked out. A year had passed since then, but it wasn't getting any easier, despite what people assured him about healing and time.

In some ways his pain was worse. He was beginning to fathom how selfish he'd been, but the realisation had come too late. Every morning he woke feeling groggy, his head aching with regret.

Michael struggled on, emerging from the track onto open sand. He trudged to a spot just above high tide mark. The gusts were stronger here, whisking the breath from his mouth. This stretch of beach belonged to him today; it was just as he'd hoped. He sat down suddenly, his whole body shaking.

He stared out at the ocean, his mind running over phrases from this morning's email: *offer you a generous redundancy package, greatly appreciate all your hard work over the years, hope you will accept our very best wishes for your future.* A bunch of false kindnesses and corny platitudes. It didn't matter now. He gripped his elbows and exhaled slowly, just as he'd learnt from the relaxation CD Sophie had given him for Christmas. The tremors in his limbs subsided. Even the wind had died away. The waves reared up, crashed and retreated.

A child's joyous shout came dancing down the beach, and Michael turned his head. The two figures were clearer, a fraction larger. He pulled his mobile from his jacket, stared at the screen, then replaced it. Standing on one leg, he began to unlace a shoe, then stopped, shaking his head. He faced the breakers, and started down to the water.

The first few steps into the surf were easy, and Michael felt strong and sure of himself. But as he waded in, his clothes became sodden and heavy. The water around his knees was so cold, his legs were wooden. His ribs vibrated, and he realised he was crying. He swiped at his cheeks with sea-wet hands. *So much salty water.* He pushed forward, the chill of the Indian Ocean creeping up to his groin.

A beeping noise rose above the churning of the sea. Michael reached for his phone. There was a new message. He laughed weakly. Why bother to read it? Yet he was curious, even now.

He shaded the screen with one hand and moved his face close to read.

Sorry Dad. You're not crap, I was just pissed off. You're a great dad, well mostly! 😁

Michael's eyes ran and he staggered with the waves, small as they were. The wide blue sky hovered attentively above him, and the sun laid its hands on his head. His breathing steadied. He looked far out to sea, to the deep navy waters, to the furthest edge of the earth – and then he turned.

~

It was almost a month before Michael could face unpacking his box of office files, books and stationery. Just the sight of his old red mug, perched on top, made him swallow. The detritus from his executive life sat on a bookcase, gathering dust.

His days were surprisingly full now. He spent his hours gardening, listening to music, walking with Sophie and cleaning out the long-neglected garage. He mowed the lawn for Doris next door whenever he did his own. He was trying his hand at watercolours. It was a strange new life, but one he was beginning to like. He had started to believe he'd work again. Maybe love again too.

The box made his back twinge as he lifted it, then huffed out office air as he thumped it onto the table. Michael stood rubbing his lower spine, regarding these workday leftovers. Poking out above the papers and books was a pale wooden frame.

Easing the painting from between folders, he pulled it free. Its familiarity was both soothing and unnerving as he ran his eyes across the seaside landscape. A split second later, Michael's eyes widened. In the middle of the canvas, crossing the sleek sand, was a trail of footprints.

With trembling hands, Michael laid the frame flat. He scanned the painting from top to bottom, but it was no trick of the light – the shoe marks were distinct and defined, as if daubed there from the very first. They led from the ocean back to dry land. The imprints were large, man-sized.

Michael stretched out a finger, touched the footsteps in amazement. A little salt water leached from his eyes, and this time he didn't wipe it away.

BIRTHDAY WISHES

I'T'S STILL EARLY, THE LIGHT gentle, the forest cool. Cypress Grove track is deserted and Ruth is grateful. She's motionless, her eyes fixed on the clearing between the trees. A thornbill twitters from a nearby bush, and tiny creatures rustle in the ferns. The smell of peat rises from the earth.

Her knees throb the way they do if she's on her feet too long, and her bladder is beginning to niggle, but Ruth is determined to ignore these discomforts. With one hand on a palm tree she takes another step, careful to place her foot without a sound.

A glossy black bird struts near two rows of short sticks rising vertically from the ground. The rows are a foot long and a hand's breadth apart. The male satin bowerbird hasn't noticed Ruth, or at least doesn't glance her way. He lifts a stick from one side and wedges it into the other, then steps back, regarding the adjustment with his indigo eyes. A second later, he darts forward and moves the twig to its original location.

Ruth smiles. She can't imagine how such fussing attracts female bowerbirds. Personally, Ruth likes a more relaxed sort of fellow. Her Kolya was always so casual – mowing only when the yard was almost overgrown, cooking lavish meals with a spoon in one hand and a glass of red in the other. Her big-boned, big-hearted Kolya.

The bird tilts its head to one side. Seeming satisfied, he begins arranging the blue objects scattered in front of the bower. He lifts a strand of royal blue twine and places it beside a turquoise plastic scrap.

Ruth leans closer, a hand on the soft flannel of Kolya's old shirt. Her husband had worn the shirt for years, until buttons began to defeat him. She'd made light of it, telling Kolya buttons were out of fashion, and bought him a thermal shirt instead. She'd kept the flannel one, couldn't bear to give it away.

The bird takes a blue straw and hops to arrange it proudly at the entrance. Squinting to admire the bird's treasures, Ruth stifles a laugh. Near the straw, there's a set of keys with a light-blue tag. Instinctively she pats her pocket for the bulge of car keys, though her own key tag is black.

A rush of wings breaks the hush as an olive-coloured bird with violet eyes lands on the edge of the circle. The male bowerbird hurries over. Seizing a bottle top, he parades before the female, offering the blue plastic like a precious gem. He whirrs and clicks as he prances to and fro, making a constant vibrating sound. Ruth doesn't dare move. She's seen satin bowerbirds many times before, but never their courtship.

The female steps into the bower, turning to inspect the walls, poking at the sticks with her beak. The male waits outside. He spreads his wings and buzzes with excitement. In a final gallant gesture, he grabs a blue feather and bows.

Ruth breathes deeply, filling her lungs. It's been ages since she's driven to Mount Glorious, and she's missed all this – the birds, the bush, the solitude. The air is crisp on her face and the sun slices pale between the trees. Today she turns eighty years old.

The black bowerbird is squawking now, plaintive cries that seem to say, *Love me! Love me!* Ruth thinks again of Kolya. There was no question of not loving that funny, cheeky man; he had no need to plead. She'd been twenty-seven, sick of blokes, thought she'd never meet a man she adored. But after several trips to the dark-eyed mechanic she'd thanked her lucky stars for her unreliable car, had been over the moon when he'd asked her out.

The discerning green bird glances at her suitor then pointedly examines his construction once more. At last she puffs out her feathers and lowers her head. She shuffles deep into the bower. The male joins her, clambering astride her back. There is a blur of flapping wings, and Ruth pushes herself off the tree, leaving them to it. She hums to herself as she walks towards the car park.

~

Ruth turns into the driveway of the post-war cottage, pulling up behind the dusty Peugeot in the carport – Kolya's reward to himself on retirement. It hasn't been driven in almost ten years now. She really must sell it – the faithful Hyundai is fine for her needs. As Ruth climbs the steps to the front door, she glances at her daughter's red Alfa Romeo, pulled tight against the kerb. Alex has inherited her father's love of cars but with a much greater income. Ruth never asks what Alex earns but it must be substantial to drive around in that machine.

The front door opens before Ruth reaches the top of the stairs.

'Hi, Mum.'

Alex looks tired, puffy beneath the eyes. She's almost fifty now, something Ruth can't quite fathom.

'How was it?' Alex asks. Her handbag is looped over her shoulder, her car keys in her hand.

Ruth takes the last two steps slowly, holding the banister. All her energy has vanished – left behind with the birds.

'Wonderful. Thank you, Alex.' She pats her daughter's arm.

'It's no problem. He's just watching TV.' Alex starts down the stairs, calling back, 'See you for dinner. We'll bring everything, don't fuss.'

Ruth waits as her daughter slides into the flashy car, then waves until she turns the corner. The shaded landing is warm. Cicadas buzz in the hedge along the fence. Across the road, Kevin Pringle is sweeping the front path in his yellow bucket hat. The *whoosh, whoosh* of the broom each morning is something Ruth relies on now, like sunrise, or the evening news.

She opens the screen door and walks into the lounge room, letting her eyes adjust. Kolya sits in the recliner chair, mouth slightly ajar. He's smaller these days, nothing like the man who would lift her in the air with his hugs. His eyes are fixed on the TV. She hurries down the hall to the loo.

~

The clock in the kitchen says it's only half past seven but conversation is slowing. Ruth knows Alex and Craig will leave soon. The four cake plates are smeared with chocolate ganache, not a bite of cake remaining. It had been a tiny, beautiful creation from an expensive patisserie; Alex put a photo on Facebook and said all her friends sent birthday wishes.

Kolya sits in his usual position at the head of the table, but he's hardly spoken. Sometimes he repeats a word or phrase, but mostly the talk drifts above him.

Alex and Craig have done their best to make the evening festive. They knew Ruth didn't want a party – all the people would have made Kolya more confused. But the food was fancy, from a local café. White balloons, each with a gold *80*, bob on the ceiling in the lounge and dining rooms. And a banner above the dining-room window reads, *Happy Birthday!*

Alex pushes her chair back. 'Well. Dishes, hey?'

Craig also rises from his chair.

Ruth waves her hand. 'No, please don't. There's hardly anything, just leave it.'

Kolya looks from face to face, his once-majestic head just skin and bone.

Alex and Craig protest, but not for long, and soon they are kissing Ruth and Kolya goodbye.

Ruth pulls Alex close. 'Thank you for making my birthday special.' It's strange to feel her daughter's body no longer lean and firm, but beginning to soften and thicken. Becoming more like her mother's.

She wonders again if Alex and Craig regret their decision not to have children, just the two of them alone forever. Ruth can't understand it – she always wanted a big family herself. It was devastating to be told she couldn't have more after Alex. But she loves her daughter, wants whatever she wants.

'No problem, Mum. Love you.' Alex kisses her cheek, and then Craig and Alex are down the stairs and driving away.

Kolya stands at the door, looking lost. If Ruth didn't know better, she'd think he was bereft. His eyes are clouded. He gazes off into the darkness.

'Who was that?'

'That was Alexandra, our daughter, and her husband, Craig.'

'Ah, yes.' Kolya nods.

'Would you like a cup of tea?' Ruth leads him to his chair, helps him settle.

'Yes. Tea.' Kolya beams, looks right at her for once, and she sees her Kolya. Then his chin drops and he burps and Ruth heads to the kitchen.

~

Ruth is weary but Kolya is wide awake and chatty. His tea is untouched. Ruth dreads nights like this, when he talks to her all hours, or roams the house, or worse – tries to go outside. She pulls the rug up around her waist. At least for now he's in his chair and she can rest on the couch.

Kolya points to the balloons, clustered near the join between ceiling and wall. 'Balloons!' He sounds delighted, a cross between a small child and the joyful Kolya of old. 'Is it someone's birthday?'

'Yes, darling, it's my birthday.' She is so tired. Her knees ache and she longs to stretch them out in bed.

'Oh!' Kolya turns to her in surprise. It must be the tenth or eleventh time that night. 'Happy birthday!'

He is quiet, studying her face. Ruth thinks lately he's not always sure who she is, though he's aware enough to realise he should know. He doesn't ever ask. The next question comes, though, like clockwork.

'How old are you?'

'I'm eighty.' She points to the balloons, with their shiny gold numerals. They're so pretty, she's got a lump in her throat.

'Well.' Kolya smiles uncertainly. 'That's very good.'

'Yes, it is,' Ruth says. She reaches across, touches his big, wrinkled hand, and Kolya turns it over, taking hers. He's forgotten so much, his memory fragmented, but he still clasps her hand as if by instinct.

Ruth thinks back through the day. She really has had a happy birthday. Cards, phone calls, a visit from her friends Margie and June. And this morning – such freedom. Those magnificent birds.

The TV burbles across the room. It's a show she likes, when she bothers to listen – a panel where contestants tell a crazy truth or an outrageous lie, and each team has to guess which it is. She loves the fibbing, loves it even more when the wildest things turn out to be true.

Kolya's grip tightens. He's staring at the drifting helium balloons.

'Is it someone's birthday?' He gestures to the ceiling, eyes wide and eager.

Ruth looks up too, at the sea of white and gold, shifting with the faintest draught.

SHINY THINGS

You've got that rush again, like being high or drunk, but you're not doing this for fun. Your hoodie drags against your body as you unlatch the side gate and peer out to the street. The stash in your pockets is worth three grand at least. Maybe more.

It's cold and dark, just a pool of light below the streetlamp a few houses up. You can barely make out the back wheel of your bike, shoved into the hedge beside the driveway. The neighbourhood is quiet. Your neck tingles as you close the gate behind you.

It's a fancy suburb, well worth the half-hour ride to get here. These Castle Hill houses are massive, with heaps of trees and fences to hide behind. You choose the ones without dogs or wireless security. Older homes are better too – thinner window panes.

There's no sign of life. No cars. But as you move away, you hear a clunk, like a door unlocking. You stop, flatten yourself against the fence.

It's amazing how many times you've seen some weirdo out at two am, rolling their bin to the kerb, or talking on their phone or just standing in the doorway, staring out. They never look happy, these people with their Mercs and Maseratis, their mansions and their triple garages, and you wonder why the fuck not. If you had that much money, you'd be stoked. You'd leave the shitty fosters now, take your sister with you, head north. You'd find a decent place to live near the water. Buy a board, learn to surf. Let Ava take ballet, like she's always wanted.

A cat yowls, then there's silence. You wonder if you imagined the sound. Sometimes you hear things when you're doing a job. Soft clicks like dog toenails coming *tap tap tap* down the hallway. A smothered cough. The clank of a deadbolt locking you inside. You hold your breath and think this is it, you're screwed. But it's never anything. You're not like those losers revved up on ice or coming down off smack. You ride here after school, scope out places where the owners are away – mailbox overflowing, lawn too long. On the night, you check for lights and knock. By August, when you turn eighteen, you'll have enough to leave with Ava.

A figure emerges from the house – the one you've just been through – and your lungs constrict. It's a woman in a nightie drifting like a ghost, not even glancing around. Your mind jumps back to the master bedroom, where you dug through the chest of drawers, the bedside tables, the walk-in closet full of dresses and silky shirts. She must have been somewhere, in one of the rooms you walked past. You'd hit the main bedroom, then the freezer, which every second moron thinks is the best place to hide their cash. After that the study, then you were out within minutes, same as every other job.

There was something off about that bedroom, though – the four-poster bed covered in pillows printed with faces. You soon realised they were all the same kid. In some he was a baby, in others he was a little kid, or older. You'd shone your torch on the centre pillow image – a guy around your age with a rich-boy grin. A bad feeling settled in your guts, and you pushed on to the kitchen. But in the desk drawers of the study, you saw the same face on a stack of papers. Above the photo were the words *KYLE DAVIS, missing since November 2012.* Below the photo, a row of the same mobile number, sideways.

The fence is hard against your shoulder blades. You take shallow breaths as the woman heads for the road, wandering across the wide front lawn. Her feet leave dark marks in the dew. She must be freezing her butt off but she doesn't shiver or cross her arms.

There's music now, thumping bass. Laughing, shouts.

She's halfway to the kerb. You creep along the side hedge.

A car is lurching down the street, the light on inside but the headlights off, people hanging out the windows, screaming. You have a sudden wish to be in that car, to be with friends instead of here, alone.

You could team up with someone, for sure; other guys do jobs in twos or threes. But they end up getting caught. Someone messes up. You can't go to juvie and leave Ava with those arseholes.

The woman's still taking zombie steps. Someone leaning out the Commodore window yells, 'Drive the fuckin car, Bronte!' Two kids are fighting for the wheel and the woman's almost at the kerb and your stomach drops away and you run like the time Ava was little and you saw her in the kitchen, reaching up to touch the flame.

You grab the nightie chick around the waist and yank her to the footpath, falling on the grass with her on top. The car goes by and someone screeches, 'Did you see that?!' but they don't stop, they're gone and the music fades. You squirm out, your back wet with dew and your neck kinked. The woman sits up, pulls her nightie down around her skinny body, twisting left and right, her eyes bugging out.

'What ...' She stands and you do too. But as you straighten, a necklace slithers from your half-open hoodie pocket. It falls to the ground, a tear-shaped diamond on a long gold chain.

The woman looks down, and you know you should run but she hasn't moved or said anything and anyway she's pathetic, has the saddest, palest face you've ever seen. There are deep lines beside her mouth. Her hair is long and messy.

'My name is Celia,' she says in a posh voice.

Your tongue is a slug and you can't take your eyes from the diamond on the grass, glinting in the shadows.

'You saved my life,' she says. 'Thank you.'

'All good,' you say at last.

Celia bends and picks up the diamond, calm as anything. 'My ex-husband gave me this.' She runs her fingers along the links. 'It's ugly, isn't it? So ostentatious.'

You're not completely sure what that means but you get the idea. Your nerves are hopping, you're still waiting for her to scream at you, or run inside shouting for the police.

'Would you like a sandwich? I'm sorry, what's your name, honey?' Celia's hand is light and cool on your arm. She smells of baby powder, like Nan. If Nan was alive, you and Ava would still be at her place, eating Anzac biscuits every day.

'Connor. No. No thanks.' You don't know why you didn't give a fake name, maybe your brain's frozen in the cold.

You back off. No way are you taking food from this freak.

Her face falls but then she calls out, 'Wait, Connor! I have steak.' She starts towards the house. 'I buy Wagyu on Fridays, in case my son comes by.'

You wonder how people can be so dumb. That kid is long gone.

The thought of steak has made your mouth water. The fosters feed you and Ava baked beans, noodles, toasties.

'Coming?' Celia's shivering now and she sounds desperate and you're really hungry. Lights have come on in the house across the road and someone's poking their head between the curtains. You decide shit, you'll take a risk. If she even touches a phone, you'll be gone. You follow her inside.

~

Celia's still talking, even though you finished your steak ten minutes ago. Under the hanging lights above the table, her crazy hair is half dark and half white, like Top Deck chocolate – the white part to her jaw, the brown part past her shoulders. She's telling some story about her ex-husband, how he used to throw a fit if his steak wasn't cooked right.

'Anyway, I guess some people are just like that. Another hash brown?' She gestures to the oven. The kitchen is different with the lights on, sparkling bright.

'Nah. Thanks.'

You need to get out of here. The diamond sits in the centre of the table.

'I'm sorry, Connor, I've been talking too much.'

Under the table, your hands clutch the pockets of your hoodie.

'Tell me about you. What's your family like?' Her forehead is all wrinkled as she asks.

You imagine telling this rich woman how your mum is an

alcoholic who couldn't deal with you and Ava. How your dad is fuck knows where, you've seen him twice in your life. That Nan saved you and Ava but then she had the stroke, and since then you've had four different fosters in the past six years. That Ava's brain is messed up from your mum drinking when she was pregnant, and you might always have to take care of your sister.

'Great,' you say, louder than you mean to. 'Dad's a plumber. Mum drives a cab. I've got an older brother, Matt. We're good mates. We play footy on the same team.'

'Oh,' Celia says. 'Well that's nice.' Her face has a funny expression and you have an urge to punch her, to smack that look away.

You stand up so quickly your chair falls over. 'I'm off.'

'Okay, Connor.' Celia gives you a watery smile.

She needs to get it together, this sad old woman. Your throat is swollen, something's tight behind your eyes.

You unzip one pocket, yank out all the jewellery you'd stuffed in with the necklace, and dump it on the table. From the other pocket, you pull out the cash and the Rolex dive watch, and shove them beside the jewellery.

'Here!' You're breathing fast, like you just ran into the room. Acid rises in your mouth and you swallow back the fatty taste of beef.

Celia glances at the pile. She reaches to touch the watch, her face even whiter than before.

After a moment, she clears the plates. She scrapes her leftovers into the bin – the steak plus most of the hash brown. Flicking on the tap, Celia squirts detergent in the sink. As the water runs, she lifts a small blue-and-white box from the benchtop.

'These tablets make me sleepwalk,' she says. She chucks the

tablets in the bin too. 'It's happened twice before, except I didn't go outside.'

Turning the water off, Celia washes a plate, stacks it in the dish rack. 'I'm sorry, Connor. You could have died, because of me.'

'No big deal,' you say. You spot a photo on the far wall – a black-and-white picture of a tall man with his arm around Celia, who is younger and actually pretty. She has both hands on the shoulders of a boy about eight or nine years old.

Celia finishes the washing up and dries her hands on her dressing-gown.

'I'm going to head,' you say, but you still don't leave.

'Alright,' Celia says. She tries to meet your gaze, but you stare at your feet. If you let her, she could turn you to stone, like the snake-hair lady in the book your nan once read to you.

'If you'd ever like to come for dinner, you'd be welcome.'

Your cheeks flame hot. 'Sure.' You give her a quick nod, this silly bitch in her fluffy robe, and you stride to the front door.

It won't open. You wrench at the doorknob, shaking the whole frame, thinking she's called the cops, kept you trapped here eating steak. Then you see there's a sliding bolt. You throw it back and open the door, gulping icy fresh air as you walk out.

You look back once, and there she is in the doorway, surrounded by yellow light. Your throat hurts so bad. You kick the mailbox on its skinny metal pole, slam it three, four times until something snaps and at last the box bends low, bowing to the ground.

~

You keep expecting sirens, or a cop car gliding up beside you, but none of that happens. It takes you half an hour to ride back

139

to Parramatta, and by the time you get there you figure you're safe.

You sneak in the back door, unlocked since you left. The house is still dark. It smells of cheese toast and cat piss. The biggest cat, Donny, comes meowing near your legs and you rub his stupid head.

You pass Ava's bedroom and peer in. She's curled beneath the blankets, just her head above the covers. A tutu is spread across the end of the bed, ready for morning. You close the door.

In the bedroom you share with that deviant Jordan, you ease yourself into the bottom bunk and drag the blankets to your chin, the black stripes of slats above you. Your insides churn with greasy food. You remember Ava in Kmart last week, how she kept pulling tutus off their hangers, how your foster mother told her, 'Put them back, greedy girl'. And to be fair, Ava's got three already – tutus you bought with your newspaper run money – but she always wants more. Different colours, Disney ones, tutus covered in those round shiny things.

You turn onto your side, slow your breathing and try to relax.

You'll head back to Castle Hill next week, find a better house. A bigger house. Buy Ava every tutu in the shop.

~

A few weeks later, you're sitting by the river with your friend Dale. Lately you've been hanging out with Dale after school instead of scoping houses. You're thinking maybe you can scrape by with what you've saved. Leave school when you turn eighteen, get a full-time job, pay for Ava that way.

The afternoon sunshine is warm on the grass. You and Dale are propped on your schoolbags, eating yesterday's iced buns you got cheap from the bakery. He's ripping bits off and feeding them to a pigeon, and you tell him bread's not good for birds and he says you're way too uptight. You're about to say at least you're not a virgin with bad breath when you see her. The woman from that night, with her Top Deck hair.

She's riding this way on an old-fashioned bike with gleaming new paintwork and a basket on the front. Her helmet is lime green and lopsided on her head. She looks like a lunatic, smiling to herself, a stream of hair blowing behind her. You half push yourself up. You could make it if you run down to the path, meet her there. But you don't move, because that would be nuts. She's no one, nobody at all.

Celia's face is rounder and her cheeks are pink. She's flying along, whipping past joggers, ringing her bell every time.

Dale says, 'You right, mate?' and you say, 'Yeah, all good' and Celia goes flashing by.

SNOWFALL

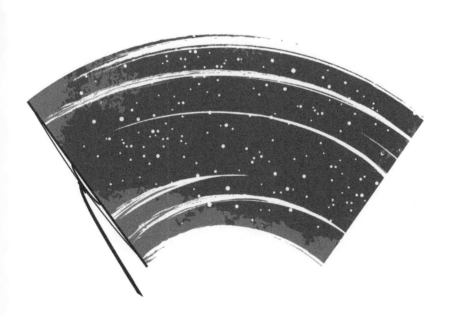

KARL PAUSED IN THE DOORWAY, tucking the old blue scarf into his coat, his wife's fine knitting soft beneath his fingers.

Outside it was snowing, the third day now. Flakes fell thick and fast, clumping wetly together before they hit the ground, swirling down under the porch light. He braced himself as he stepped outside.

'Drive safely now, Dad.' Bridget waited on the doorstep. 'The roads are going to be messy.' She reached to hug him again, and he allowed the embrace, patting her arm with his glove. Her face against his was warm and damp.

As she drew back, she touched his sleeve. 'Are you sure you don't want to stay?'

Karl imagined being tucked up in the guest room, the heating so high that he needed just one blanket, waking in the morning to oatmeal with raisins, expensive coffee and the banter of his teenage grandchildren. There would be laughter and fresh bananas and those extravagant thick towels Bridget liked to buy.

If he drove to his small house the next suburb over, he'd wake in the tidy bedroom with Annie smiling from the frame beside him and the terrible, snowy silence.

But Walter, Bridget's husband, hovered in the hall with his pear-shaped belly and dopey smile. Karl stepped away. He was too tired for Walter's kindness.

'I'm fine. You go inside, get warm. Goodnight.'

'Night, Dad. Call us when you get home.'

The yellow wedge of light followed Karl down the shovelled path, already dusted white. Taking short, careful steps, he turned along the sidewalk. The street was lined with cars – a party somewhere, he supposed – but at least he'd found a spot outside the house next door.

The Volvo's windshield was filmed over and he swiped the fresh snow with his forearm then eased himself in, tucking his legs behind the wheel. At last Bridget and Walter disappeared inside.

He turned the ignition. Nothing. Tried again. Nothing.

'Mein Gott!'

He hauled himself out and back to the house, up the four steps to the front stoop. The doorbell wasn't working – that dummkopf Walter never remembered to change the batteries – so he knocked loudly, just like before, cold wood grazing his knuckles. He crossed his arms as he waited. He'd have to call roadside assistance; no use asking Walter for help.

Though he'd dressed in layers, the Vancouver winter chill seeped through coat and sweater, through shirt and undershirt. He shuddered, and stamped his feet. After a minute, he tried the door and was relieved to find it unlocked.

He hurried into the balmy foyer, where the smell of beef stroganoff lingered. Walter was playing music in the kitchen – a beige, bland melody, something a dentist might play in

146

their waiting room. Karl had tried giving him better CDs –
Tchaikovsky, Wagner, Shostakovich – but though Walter thanked
him, he kept playing the same old scheisse.

'Hal-lo!' Karl slipped his gloves into his pockets, and bent to
remove his shoes.

A pot clanged into the sink and water blasted from a tap.

'God I'm exhausted.'

It was Bridget, speaking loudly over the clatter. No wonder
she was weary, his poor girl, being married to Walter.

'He drives me crazy,' Bridget half shouted.

Karl straightened slowly. The warmth was returning to his
fingers and ears. Bridget said something else, her words muffled
by the rattle of cutlery.

'He's alright. You just have to listen. That's all he wants.'
Walter was such a dull man, a man who baked cakes and spoke
in clichés.

'But that's the problem. That's all you *can* do with Dad. He
sure as hell won't listen. He just wants to talk, talk, talk.'

He'd never heard his daughter like this. Forceful. Vicious,
almost.

'He's not interested in anyone else. Think about it, Walt.
When did he last ask you anything?'

There was only music from the kitchen. Karl pictured his son-
in-law shrugging his shoulders.

'Exactly. You can't remember.'

Karl was breathing faster, leaning against the wall. He had one
shoe back on and he pressed his right foot into the other, always
harder because of the bunion on that side. The heat in the house
was ridiculous; he was sweating like a Swede in a sauna.

'Well, if you … then why … every Sunday night?' Only

fragments came through as Walter moved about the kitchen. Karl twisted his foot feverishly against the leather. The shoe was so tight. A muscle twinged in his lower back.

'Because he's lonely. Because since Mom died, he's like a lost boy.' Bridget's tone was less strident, more like the daughter he knew – or thought he knew.

'And anyway I have to. He's my dad.'

Karl shoved his foot violently into place and left the house without tying his laces, closing the door behind him.

~

Out in the car it was bitter. He shivered as he pulled his cell phone from the glove compartment. The battery was almost flat, but it would do the job. He pressed buttons with cold–clumsy fingers, starting again several times.

'Hello, it's Walter.' Sing-song Walter. Insipid music warbled in the background.

'Karl here. Just signing in.' He clenched his jaw to stop it juddering.

'Oh, great. You're home, then?'

'Safe and sound. Goodnight.' He tossed the phone onto the passenger seat. He didn't want them barging out here, bossing him around, taking over. Helping him out of duty. Out of pity. He sat staring through the windshield. The street was quiet and the snow had stopped. The streetlamp nearby glowed thinly above houses and parked cars.

At the neighbour's house beside him, old Mrs Yuki opened her door and tottered onto the porch. Her scrappy little dog scurried down the steps to run circles on the lawn, skidding and sliding, kicking up snow in delight.

Tears gathered behind his eyes.

He pulled out his wallet and found the roadside assist card. The car was as cold as a tomb but still he sat gripping the hard plastic. Mrs Yuki called her dog and they disappeared inside.

Karl gazed across white lawns, frosted trees, snowy roofs. He recalled a winter maybe ten years ago, well before Annie got sick. For six days the city had been decked out like a bride, and his wife had been so thrilled, while he'd stomped around complaining about shovelling snow. It made him queasy now to think of it.

The card warped in his hand. He reached for the phone, only to see the screen flash one final battery image then go black.

Across the lawn, Bridget and Walter's porch light flicked off and the living room darkened. Moments later, the master bedroom lit up behind curtains.

In the basement, every window blazed like a lighthouse. They were nice enough, his grown-up grandkids, but spoilt. Like tonight – they'd said goodbye as he was putting on his coat and then disappeared downstairs, leaving all the dirty dishes; Sam cradling a second bowl of strudel and Ella dragging that foreigner boyfriend.

The night air had found his bones. His whole body was shaking. He felt about on the back seat for the picnic rug Annie had always kept there 'just in case'. It was musty and stiff, with the faint smell of oranges. He wrapped it around himself.

Oh, Annie.

The snowfall had begun again, slipping from the sky in tiny shining pieces. His hands and feet were numb. He supposed he should cross the street, bang on the door, cause a commotion, annoy his daughter again. He pulled the blanket tighter.

His eyelids were heavy. He'd stayed later than usual, telling them all about the day he started school. His memories were vivid as a movie – trailing his brother down the narrow street in Essen, the cold air nipping at his earlobes; the smiling soldier who'd winked at him; the distant drone of planes. He'd thought his family would want to hear, but they'd just nodded with glazed eyes. Bridget had yawned behind her hand, which made him keep talking. Perhaps he'd told them once before. Still, they should show some respect. That boyfriend of Ella's had listened, but he was an Arab. Egyptian parents, he'd said. Karl was never sure about those Arabs.

There was no one in the world like Annie. He knew that now.

Most of the houses were in darkness. An odd warmth began in Karl's chest, spreading outwards like rays of sun. He closed his eyes.

~

Bridget rubbed cream into her elbows as she sat on the edge of the bed.

'I hope Dad's asleep. I hope he's not sitting in his recliner playing Beethoven in the dark.'

Walter rinsed his mouth and spat into the ensuite sink. 'He's fine. He sounded fine when he called.' He glanced in the mirror, running his hand through his thinning hair before strolling to his side of the bed.

Bridget slipped under the covers beside him. 'What did he say?'

Walt reshaped his pillow. 'I don't remember. Just that he was alright.'

'Okay.' She opened her mouth then closed it again. She switched off the lamp. 'Goodnight.'

'Night.'

They lay on their backs. The snow made the night unusually bright. The streetlight shone through a crack in the curtains, cutting across the foot of their bed.

'Walt?'

'Yes?' His voice was patient.

'Did he say anything about dinner, about the food?'

There was a brief silence. 'No, hon.'

'No. Of course.' She rubbed her face with her hands.

'But, you know, he was on his cell. So he didn't chat.'

Bridget's hands stilled. 'On his cell?'

'Yah. I noticed on the caller ID.'

'Why would he call on his cell? He hates that thing. Hates the cost.'

'Well, he did. The old dog's got new tricks.'

Bridget sat up. 'I'm serious, Walt. Why would he use his cell at home?'

Walter groaned. 'I don't know. I have no idea. I do know that it's –' he leant to consult the clock '– eleven twenty-three.' He tucked the pillow under his neck, turning on his side.

Bridget shunted back beneath the duvet. 'Don't you think that's weird, though?'

There was no reply. Walt's breathing slowed and deepened. Soon he began to snore.

Bridget twisted away, patting the surface of the bedside table until she found her earplugs. Eventually she, too, was taking long, scraping breaths, like a shovel rasping through snow.

~

Ella and Maged lay snuggled on the couch in the basement. On the TV, Phoebe from *Friends* was getting married – a snowy winter wedding.

Maged grunted and reached for the remote.

'No way!' Ella slid to the end of the couch, holding the device aloft.

Maged growled, rising to his knees, and was leaning to kiss her when Sam burst from the bathroom in a cloud of steam, a towel around his waist.

'Guys. Could you take it somewhere else?'

'Get a life. You're just jealous.' Ella made a rude gesture to Sam's retreating back.

Maged settled beside her. He picked up her hand and toyed with her fingers. Onscreen, the wedding continued.

'So, what did your Opa think of me?'

'I'm sure he liked you. He's just set in his ways.'

'What does that mean?' Maged released Ella's hand.

'He's not good with some things.'

'Like?'

'Well, you know. You're Egyptian.'

'Actually, I'm Canadian.' He shifted away.

'You know what I mean.'

'So, what? Karl doesn't like Egyptians, blanket rule?'

'He's old. I don't think he can change.' Ella laid a hand on his leg.

Maged got up and crossed the room. He slid a book from the shelf, then replaced it. 'Did he say something? About me?'

'No. But we didn't talk. *He* talked. You saw what he's like.'

Maged turned. 'Yah. It's not so much conversation. More like a lecture.'

Ella sighed. 'Pretty much.'

'So, he hogs the conversation, he has a problem with Egyptians. How come you adore him?'

'Well, he's more than just those things.'

Her boyfriend was silent.

'Maged.' Ella got up and hugged him. 'I'm sorry. He's a racist old man. But he's my Opa too.'

Maged nodded. 'Yah, I know.' He rubbed her back. 'I guess I should go. I've got hockey early.' He grabbed his coat from the armchair. 'Tell Sam I said bye.'

'Okay.' Ella followed him upstairs to kiss him at the door.

~

Maged carried the warmth of the kiss into the cold, still night. Before Ella, winter nights made him lonely. Now he went around in a bubble, protected from discomfort. The sub-zero air didn't touch him.

He whistled as he fished car keys from his pocket, glad to see his Corolla down the road only lightly covered in snow. One car closer was a boxy old Volvo. At dinner, Sam had teased Karl about the ancient car.

Maged slid the keys back into his pocket. The hairs on his neck feathered up, but for a moment he did nothing. His breath fogged in the air. Nothing moved. There was no sound. Even the powerline hum was smothered by the snow.

In four steps he was at the passenger window, scraping slush with his fingers. Someone was slumped in the driver's seat.

Maged scrambled around, heart pounding. He opened the door and Karl toppled sideways, wrapped in some kind of rug.

'Oh, Jesus.' Maged reached in and propped Karl upright.

The old man's eyes were closed and he didn't respond, but his shoulders lifted as he breathed and his neck was warm. Maged scanned the neighbourhood for someone, anyone. It was a long way to the house – too far to lug the lanky old man on his own. Maged pulled out his cell and dialled 911.

After the call, Maged looped the rug around Karl's shoulders and tugged him from the car, holding him chest to chest like a lover. He propped the old man on the Corolla to unlock it, lowered Karl into the seat and shut the door.

Racing to the driver's side, Maged jumped in and cranked up the heat. He pulled the blanket around Karl and watched him breathe, taking a big, cold hand between his own.

The hatchback was warming up.

'Karl? Can you hear me?'

Karl turned his head slightly, hair mussed by the rug. His eyes were bleary but his lips had changed from blue to mauve.

'Are you alright?' Maged peered closer.

Karl blinked and looked around. 'Yes. I'm alright.' He spoke slowly.

Maged nodded. 'Good. You look better. We're in my car, okay? Till the ambulance comes.'

He wondered if he should be doing something else. Hugging him? Using his own body warmth? He glanced up into watery blue eyes.

Karl clutched the edges of the blanket. 'What are your ... plans ... with Ella?'

Maged laughed, loose with relief. He thought he heard a siren, faint as an echo.

'Well, sir, that depends on her. But I hope we'll get married one day.' It was hot now in his down-filled coat and sheepskin-lined boots. He wiped sweat from his forehead.

'She can't … marry you. You're Egyptian.' Karl's speech was clear now. He sat forward, the first real movement since Maged had found him curled stiff in the car seat.

Maged's blood surged then subsided. He'd been through this crap so many times.

'Actually, I'm Canadian.'

The siren was louder, definitely close.

Karl appeared not to hear, muttering to himself.

Maged moved closer. 'What was that?'

The old man turned, exhaled garlic breath. 'I said – funny-looking Canadian.'

The car was tropical inside, so much heat for a nasty old man. Maged was cooking in his jacket, anger bubbling across his skin.

The ambulance appeared at the corner, its howl deafening in the sleeping street, lights flicking red across the snow. Maged jumped from the car.

'Here! Over here!' He waved his arms above his head. The ambulance switched off the siren, pulling in just past the Corolla.

Lights began to dot the street and shadowy figures appeared at windows and on doorsteps. Bridget rushed out in a dressing-gown as paramedics shifted Karl to a stretcher, covering him in blankets and foil. Walter raced to Bridget's side with a coat, Sam close behind.

Ella ran to Maged. 'God, what happened? What was he doing out here?'

Maged shook his head. He followed Karl to the ambulance.

The older paramedic gave Maged a quick smile. 'You did a good job. Warmed him up well. He should be fine.'

Maged nodded, releasing a long, slow breath.

Bridget clung to Walter, her face stricken.

Maged stepped closer, a hand on the foil. The old man turned his head, waved Maged closer till he bent to hear. Seconds later, the paramedics slid the stretcher in and closed the doors.

As the ambulance drove away, Ella's family hurried towards the house, discussing who would drive Bridget to the hospital.

Ella wound her arm through Maged's, her whole body quaking. 'What did Opa say?'

Maged blinked in the glare of the porch light, holding back a nervous laugh. 'He said, "Get inside, it's cold".'

~

Karl poked a fork at the mound of yellow. 'This is not scrambled egg.'

His fourth-floor room was filled with the winter dawn light.

Bridget looked up. 'What?' She was sitting beside the bed, fiddling with her phone.

'Nothing. Don't worry. I'm only your father, speaking to you.' He jabbed at the cold, rubbery food. It seemed that this schreckliche meal was all that was wrong with the world.

'Dad! I'm texting Walter to come get us.' She didn't look up as she rebuked him, her cheeks crinkled near her mouth. It struck him that even she was getting old.

Karl pushed the table tray away from his bed. 'Sure, sure. Do whatever. You all do whatever.' He knew he was acting like a child but he couldn't seem to stop.

Bridget put her phone down, suddenly intense. 'You know, you almost *died*. If it wasn't for Maged …' She frowned. 'Are you even grateful?'

Karl remembered the warm, sleepy feeling the evening before, when all sadness had faded away. Then blankness, until the boy appeared.

'I'm grateful.' He felt a twinge of guilt. Ella's friend seemed like a good boy. Karl would write, thank the boy the way he should have.

He scrunched the blanket in his hands. 'But you? Are you?'

'What are you talking about?' Bridget's eyebrows drew together and she reminded him of Annie when he'd annoyed her.

He shrugged. 'Are you glad I didn't die?'

'What? Of course!'

Karl swung his legs around. The linoleum was cool beneath his feet.

'I heard you, you know. After dinner.' He shuffled to the cupboard, removed his shirt and pants from the hanger and laid both items on the bed. He began undoing his pyjama buttons. 'I came to the door but you didn't hear me.'

Bridget's hand rose to her throat. 'Oh, Dad.'

His eyes stung, like when he'd watched that idiotic dog next door. He slid one arm in, then the other, and shrugged into the shirt. The buttons were tiny and slippery; it took him forever to do up the six pearly circles.

'Whatever I said, Dad, I didn't mean it. I was tired and grumpy.'

Karl adjusted the collar and smoothed the shirt down. 'You don't think I talk too much?'

His daughter dropped her head. 'Well, yes. You do, a bit.'

He undid the pyjama tie and let the pants fall to the floor, sitting back on the hospital bed in shirt and underwear.

He picked up his trousers and held them in front, stepping one foot and then the other into the legs. He stood and smoothed his shirt into the pants before zipping up.

Bridget passed him the belt. 'I'm sorry, Dad.'

He looked at her and nodded. 'I'm a difficult man, I know this. Your mother also knew. But anyway she loved me.' He coughed and looked around for his shoes.

Outside the window, golden sun spilled across buildings and parklands. Snow lingered on rooftops and trees, but it would be gone in a couple of days.

'I love you too.' Bridget's voice was unsteady. The skin beneath her eyes was puffy and her hair was tangled. He realised she'd been up for most of the night.

'Here, Dad.' She held out the brogues, her gaze gentle as a prayer.

'Danke.' Karl sat back on the bed, shoes in his lap. He felt quite well.

When they dropped him home, his Bridget and her husband, he'd ask them inside. There was fancy French Roast in the cupboard, a pack Karl had purchased for the next time they stopped by.

He'd collect the mail, feed the bird and change into his slippers. After that, he'd make coffee for them all.

PITTER-PATTER

SHE'D BEEN HEARING IT ALL afternoon, ever since Anthea and Brock had driven away with the baby in the back – tooting as they rounded the corner, a haze of dust hanging in the air. Megan had dropped her arm mid-wave, standing in front of the old stone house. She wondered if the faint chattering was real, or something in her ears. Wax, or water from her swim yesterday, at home.

She'd unpacked, eaten lunch, tried to journal. Wandered around the scraggly veggie garden with Roxy following, panting in the heat. The noise caught her attention, then disappeared. As the sun lowered, she'd thrown scraps into the chook pen, fed Roxy. Tossed hay over the fence for the skinny sheep – bales Brock had left out in the yard.

In the waning light, she sat on the front doorstep. Galahs screeched past, flying west. Something rustled in the dry patch of lawn – a lizard or a skink she supposed. Megan thought of Juan, probably making dinner right now. Steak and chimichurri, or just a sandwich, since it was only him. Guilt twinged in her gut. He was hurting too, she knew that. But it was different for him, she was sure. It wasn't his body failing them, not his body that couldn't sustain a child.

Roxy nudged Megan's hands, and she rubbed behind the cattle dog's ears. The air was rich with the scent of sun-baked grass. In the distance, a stray sheep trotted to catch up with the others. The sky gradually turned purple and a few stars appeared. Megan watched as more emerged, each speck growing brighter. Back in Adelaide, she rarely noticed the stars.

The beginnings of comfort settled in her bones. This week would be good for everyone. Anthea and Brock could have a proper holiday, and it would be a break for her too. No clients hassling her about events. No Juan, with his disappointed face – last month, the month before that, every month the past seven years, his sadness compounding her own.

Now she heard it again – high-pitched and indistinct, like a schoolyard full of children. She sat forward, her forehead tight. Was she losing her mind? She angled her head towards the noise, but it became softer then was gone. The house, the yard, the paddocks all around were still. Megan waited, tensed like a runner at the start line.

In the twilight, with every building, fence and bush turned to shadows, her sense of isolation grew. She recalled the contact details, stuck on the fridge, for Anthea and Brock's nearest neighbour. Brock had said Hans was 'just six ks down the road' and she'd pretended to find that reassuring.

She shivered, and hurried inside.

~

Megan read over the words she'd just written.

Sometimes I think I can't bear it, but of course, I do.

She got up and poured more tea. She'd started the journal to deal with the IVF. Anthea was great, and had been through IVF too, but she was busy with her life out here. Other friends couldn't understand, not fully. When Megan was with them, there were strange undercurrents. The women talked about anything besides their children, in halting, awkward conversations. And despite their consideration, irritation would rise inside her. The sight of their smooth-skinned babies made her prickle and itch. In her darker moments, she longed to slap her friends' smug, happy cheeks.

Leaning against the bench, Megan sipped the lukewarm Earl Grey. The grandfather clock ticked sternly in the lounge room. She replayed the discussion with Juan last week. They'd decided enough was enough. No more injections, no more egg harvests, no more tests.

She ditched her tea in the sink and dialled Juan, the buttons on the landline odd beneath her fingers. Mobile reception was patchy out here – a good thing, she'd decided. She'd have a digital detox. Detox from everything.

The phone rang, hollow and distant, over and over. Megan gripped the handset, the lingering taste of Earl Grey too floral in her mouth. She was sure, suddenly, that Juan was with another woman. Amy from his office. Amy with her sleek blonde hair, who laughed all the time. Amy who could give him children.

Juan answered, his voice so close and warm that tears sprang into Megan's eyes. She blinked them back and asked about his day. Eventually, a gap opened in their conversation.

'So, there's a sound out here.' Megan stopped, considered changing the subject to something cheerful and amusing. But she had to tell someone. 'It comes and goes. Like a bunch of kids all talking at once.'

'That's weird,' Juan said.

'I know.' Megan scratched a mosquito bite so hard the skin broke, and it bled. She pulled a tissue from the box beside the fridge.

'Are you alright?' he asked, his tone light.

'Of course,' she replied. She blotted the red from her thigh.

'Well, lock up, go to bed. Don't read too late.'

'Mmm.' It annoyed her when he told her what to do, even if it made sense. 'Goodnight.'

Megan wandered down the hall. She'd been up at five, on the road by six. It would be good to have an early night.

She showered and brushed her teeth, then slid into bed. There was no clock in the bedroom – Anthea said she and Brock always woke to the birds or the baby. After two pages of her book, Megan clicked off the lamp.

Darkness rushed into the room, thick and oppressive. She held out her hands and waited for her eyes to adjust, but the blackness did not recede. The clock chimed in the living room, marking the hour with solemn strokes. When it finished, she was sure she could hear ticking, even here in the bedroom. She rolled onto her side, pulling a pillow across her head.

~

Megan woke in the pitch black, her tongue dry as a rock and her heart alarming. For a moment, she had no idea where she was, then she remembered. Brock's family farm. Anthea's home now too. Out past Kimba, the middle of nowhere.

In the dense, dark night, she felt invisible, disembodied. Her pulse wouldn't slow. She told herself to snap out of it. She was safer here than in Adelaide, by far.

Roxy yapped sharply, out behind the house. Megan sat up. Anthea had warned her not to be scared, told her that Roxy barked at snakes, roos, wallabies – any animals that came near the house.

Megan fumbled with the bedside light. The barking continued, spiking under her skin. She felt for the switch in the hall, and made her way into the kitchen. Tucking the spotlight under her arm, she unlocked the back door.

The beam swung across the yard, side to side. Once or twice she thought she saw something, a shimmer of movement, but when she looked again, there was nothing. She lowered the spotlight.

'Roxy! Here, Roxy!'

The dog didn't appear. Megan trained the torch on the kennel, and a pair of eyes flashed back. Megan crept across the yard, more dirt than grass, wary of creatures underfoot.

'Hey, girl, what's up?' The dog thumped her tail on the kennel floor. Megan could see her wider girth now she was lying down. Anthea had explained Roxy had gone missing for the day a while ago, and recently they'd realised she was pregnant, due in a couple of weeks. Roxy stretched her front legs, her paws jutting out through the doorway. She looked placid and unconcerned.

Megan crossed her arms against the chill. 'No more barking, okay?'

The dog glanced away, used to whistles and a few sharp words, Megan guessed, not rambling conversation.

Megan retraced her steps and crawled into bed. This time she was prepared for the blackness, but she found herself wired and awake. She lay on her back, counting breaths. Her thoughts began to splinter from reality.

Something went pattering down the hall, just outside the room. It was light and quick, like a tiny baby running. Megan's skin rippled with goosebumps. She was afraid to move. Seconds passed as she listened. The house was silent.

There was no goddamn baby, not in the hall and not inside her. Grief came howling in, that unbearable scouring pain. She curled in a ball, and waited for the agony to subside.

~

'How was your night?' Juan asked. Megan had woken to the ringing phone with sunshine on the bed, and Roxy whining at the back door.

'Good, all good.' Megan tipped kibble into the round steel bowl, and clicked her fingers to tell Roxy she could eat. The memory of the running baby filled her head, vivid and alive, as if she'd really seen it racing down the hall.

'So what will you do today?'

She leant against the doorframe as the dog scoffed the food in a matter of seconds. 'I don't know. Do the chores. Walk. Think.' The chooks cackled in their pen. Just beyond the yard, the stand of mallee scrub swayed in the wind.

'Well. Don't think too much, hey?' Juan often did this, trying to steer them both to safety. For the past seven years, his approach had helped, but she needed to adjust to this decision. Juan didn't want to adopt; he said at fifty, he couldn't face another long process. She would turn forty next year and most of her agreed. Being childless wouldn't ruin them – they'd still have a happy and fulfilling life. But it would take her time to believe this.

'Talk to you later,' Megan said, and they hung up.

She wandered through the house. The place was friendly again, bright with the morning. In the kitchen, Megan stopped at the window to watch a magpie perched on the tank ladder, tilting its head as if listening intently. High above, a streak of cloud drifted east.

She opened kitchen drawers and cupboards, and peered at prints in the living room. Running her fingers along the buffet, she picked up photos and set them gently down. In Tucker's room, she sat in the rocking chair. A scuffed pair of toddler sandals lay abandoned beneath the dresser. Small wooden boats dangled over the cot – blue, red and yellow, shifting slightly. Now and then, they touched with a click. A sweet baby smell lingered.

Megan rocked onto her feet. Back in the kitchen, she removed the contents of the pantry. She sprayed and wiped each shelf, the cloth darkening with grime, then replaced the items. She did the same with the fridge, and the rest of the kitchen drawers and cupboards. After lunch, she vacuumed the whole house, beads of sweat running down her temples. Finally, she mopped the floors, then took a long, cold shower. Stepping out of the old clawfoot bath, she was tired but calm.

At five o'clock, in fresh clothes, Megan pulled a battered hat from the peg behind the back door. 'C'mon, Rox,' she called. The dog leapt up from a spot of shade.

She headed for the big shed, Roxy by her side. Brock had taken the last of the hay from the small open shed, and the sheep needed extra feed. Megan hummed softly to herself. It was cooler this afternoon, the thermometer in the house already dropping into the teens. *Crazy place, crazy weather,* Anthea had said in an email after she moved out here.

Spotting the water tank, Megan changed direction. The tank

was the farm's highest point – it was bound to have a view. The sheep could wait.

She hauled herself up the ladder. Roxy watched, her tongue hanging out. On the roof, Megan planted herself in the centre. The parched, barren land spread out before her – a gentle slope upwards from road to house, flattening out behind the home paddock. The sun dangled low, a blazing gold. Megan turned full circle. Out here, sky and earth were boundless.

Roxy gave an impatient yip, and Megan smiled. She clambered down the ladder and walked on.

The dog stopped. She growled. Megan rested a hand on Roxy's scruff. 'What's up?'

She could hear it again, same as yesterday. She shook her head, wondering once more about her ears. But the noise became insistent as she tramped towards the shed. Roxy led the way, tail at high alert.

Something flickered in Megan's vision to the left, then to the right. Her nerves jumped, until she saw it was just a mouse, scampering in the grass. Roxy barked.

'Roxy, it's just a mouse,' Megan said. But she couldn't relax and something nagged at her brain. There was a thick, musky stench. Her ears filled with chirping and cheeping, and the realisation came as she opened the shed door.

Mice poured out, flowing like syrup, leaping over the doorjamb. They chittered and squawked, jumping from walls and dropping from the centre beam. One ran up her leg and she screamed, swiping it away. Roxy bellowed her outrage, dashing about in the sea of mice. Megan left the door ajar and stumbled towards the house, treading on squishy bodies as she went.

Within moments she felt claws on her hand, a wriggling in her gumboots. 'You fuckers,' she yelled, beating at her body, her arms and legs. Something tangled in her hair and she shrieked, pulling the creature from behind her ear, flinging it to the ground.

As she neared the house, Megan glanced back. Roxy stood by the shed, pacing and barking. A mouse raced along her tail before diving off, soon replaced by another. Roxy shook her coat and whimpered, her eyes beseeching.

'Roxy, *come!*' Megan called, swatting and swearing as she ran the last few steps.

She reached the door with Roxy, pushed the dog inside and banged the door closed. A few mice went scuttling under the stove and down the hall. Megan threw her boots into a corner and saw a mouse dash beneath the buffet. Roxy paced. She seemed uncertain what to do in this forbidden place.

'Here, girl.' Megan returned from the linen press, placing a folded blanket near the back door. Roxy flopped down, nose resting on her legs.

Megan sat beside the dog, leaning on the wall. She could still feel the mice underfoot, the squirming, writhing flesh. Could hear the squealing as she'd opened the shed door. Could still smell the putrid mix of urine and fur.

She wanted to ring Juan. Then Anthea. But first she would shower off the crawling, rinse the stink from her hair. Find composure. She needed them both to know she could handle this. She'd do some research, then call.

~

At nine-thirty that night, Megan rolled the chair back from the desk. The internet was slow, but she knew a lot more about mice. She'd read of their immense capacity to reproduce, their ability to fit through tiny holes. Plagues occurred mostly in autumn, when hordes of hungry mice descended on farms, sometimes literally overnight. Also, mice liked hay.

She felt better knowing the options for mouse control. But it was too late to disturb farm folk. She'd call Anthea and Brock in the morning.

Megan made herself a sandwich and fed Roxy. She let the dog outside to pee, then called her back to the makeshift bed. It was silly, Megan knew, but she wanted Roxy inside, wanted her close.

She sat at the kitchen bench to call Juan, ready to tell him everything. He'd be appalled on her behalf; he had a horror of vermin of any kind. But as his number buzzed, she remembered he was at an important work dinner, and she missed him for the first time this trip. She left a voice message: *So, I found the noise. Ring me later?* Just before she hung up, she added, *Love you.*

~

The grandfather clock chimed seven times. Megan climbed out of bed, tipped her gumboots upside down, then slipped her feet into the boots. She'd been wearing them everywhere, just in case.

Beyond the bathroom window, sheep clustered near the fence. *They're hungry,* she thought. She would get their hay.

She entered the kitchen and stopped. Roxy lay like a crescent, two small bodies beside her. One puppy wormed around, crying softly. The other was silent, motionless.

'Oh, Roxy.' Megan crouched on her heels.

Roxy raised her head. The old blanket beneath her was dark with blood, a patch the size of a bread plate. Megan shuffled towards Roxy's tail end, but there was no sign of further bleeding.

'You right, girl?'

The dog's tail lifted and fell, a single beat. She laid her head back down.

'I'm going to check your babies, okay?' Megan sat beside Roxy. She reached out, inch by inch, until she touched the still, slick puppy. It was cool already, and there was no fast flutter beneath its breastbone.

'I'm sorry, Rox.' Megan wiped her cheeks in the crook of her elbow.

Roxy watched with weary eyes.

Megan edged her hand across to the snuffling black-and-white pup. It was warm and soft and round. The puppy rubbed its head blindly on Roxy's flank.

'He wants a drink, girl.' Megan eased Roxy's baby along so its mouth lined up with a teat. It bobbed and nodded, until finally it latched on and drank. Roxy sighed, closing her eyes. The puppy drank in muffled, rhythmic gulps, paws resting on its mother's belly.

Megan sat cross-legged beside them, hardly breathing.

~

As Anthea and Brock pulled up, Megan was shovelling another wheelbarrow load of limp grey bodies into a plastic bin. She'd placed the baited wheat up high, as Brock had suggested, avoiding risk to Roxy. Today Megan had fetched more hay for the sheep, and several mice had shot off in all directions, but there'd been no torrent like on Sunday.

'You're amazing,' Anthea said as they hugged hello. 'Anyone else would have bailed.'

'Oh, I don't give up without a fight,' Megan said, her throat clogged. She clasped her friend a moment longer.

Brock lifted Tucker from the car seat, holding the boy against his chest. 'Thanks a lot. Seriously.'

Roxy was there too, her tail whacking Anthea's legs and her mouth wide with joy as she ran to Brock. But before he could pat her, she disappeared around the back.

'How's the pup?' Anthea said. She reached for Tucker, and propped him on her hip.

'Gorgeous. Good. Thriving, far as I can tell.' Megan tried to rein in her gushing.

'And have you named him yet?' Brock opened the front door for Anthea and Megan.

Megan followed her friend inside. 'Not really.' She paused, thinking of all the hours she'd watched the little guy sleeping, or feeding, or pulling himself around. 'I've been calling him Pudding.'

Brock gave a snort of amusement and Anthea smirked.

'He's just so roly-poly.' Megan's cheeks grew warm. A working dog needed a sensible name, she knew that.

Anthea set Tucker on his feet, and he toddled down the hall. Brock trailed after his son.

'Well, you've got naming rights,' Anthea said. 'Just don't forget to collect him in nine weeks' time.'

Megan stared. 'What?'

Anthea poured herself a glass of water from the tap. 'He'll be ready to leave his mother by then.'

'Don't you want him?' Megan's voice was unsteady.

Anthea swallowed a mouthful. 'Nah. Brock says one dog is enough, and two is double the vet bills. Pudding's all yours.'

Megan nodded. She wouldn't ask Juan – she'd let him know. It was her turn to decide for them both.

Anthea fiddled with her glass, tracing a finger around the base. 'You've had a rough time. I'm really sorry.'

'You have too. The drought, and the bloody mice.' Megan looked at her friend. 'But yeah. Thank you.'

Tucker came tripping down the hall, and buried his head into Anthea's leg.

'Megan's going to take Pudding,' Anthea said to Brock as he returned.

'Good.' He touched Megan's shoulder, then strode out towards the car. 'Good!' he called back.

Anthea's fingers rested in Tucker's curly hair.

A magpie chortled from the clothes line, the notes ringing out like an announcement.

A SLOW EXHALATION

As LINCOLN DROVE OUT OF Goulburn, the shops and houses thinned away and turned to farmland. His shoulders dropped and his jaw unclenched, despite what he'd done last night. He wound down the window and let the air blow in, a sweet mix of grass and cow pats.

He imagined Kate right now, hugging her parents outside the café, her mum and dad in their fine Sydney clothes. 'Yeah, he had to work,' Kate might say. Or maybe she'd tell the truth, just say it straight out: 'We broke up last night.' She'd put up with him for half a year, but in the end he'd done what he always did, finished things before the girlfriend could. It was better that way.

The road rose upwards and trees huddled either side. Lincoln leant an elbow on the door, the ute's vibrations a familiar comfort. He'd be alright. Life would go on. He'd go to work and mow ovals, sweep paths, spray weeds. Say hello to Max and Shaz when they arrived to clean the classrooms. Head home to his flat each night and have a few beers. Cook bangers and mash, or walk to the pub for a countery, talk to Stan and some of the other old fellas who practically lived there.

The sign for Bungonia National Park appeared, and Lincoln flicked his indicator. The bushland was dense with trees and scrub. He drove to the middle car park, pulled into a space and strode to the boot.

The sun was bright but the breeze was cool. The car park was almost empty, just a few other cars and no one in sight.

The track leading to Fossil Cave was quiet too. Trees blocked most of the midday sunshine and already Lincoln felt a chill, as if the cave air was reaching out to greet him. It reminded him of when he'd first gone caving ten years ago, with his high school friend Dom. Dom's dad had stopped them at the narrow mouth of a cave and told them to kneel, to put their faces to the entrance. They'd hunched together, their mocking eyes meeting, until they felt something against their cheeks – a slow, steady exhalation.

'It's called cave breathing,' Dom's dad told them. 'If the outside air pressure is low, the cave breathes out. If it's high, the cave draws air in.'

Lincoln had felt a tingling in his arms, a rippling excitement. He'd been caving ever since.

Now he turned off the track.

The entrance to Fossil Cave was neat, with a metal platform and an iron ladder that disappeared down the gap between boulders. Except for the absence of signs, it looked like a tourist cave, something to wander through in an hour.

Lincoln unzipped his bag and pulled on his helmet. He remembered the last time he'd gone potholing, when Kate had finally agreed to come. She'd clowned around on the platform, posing in her helmet, until he'd smiled, switched on her headlamp and moved down the ladder.

Lincoln swung the backpack onto his shoulders. He turned

to descend, gripping the ladder, feeling his footing. This was his favourite part of solo caving – the pure escape of it, how he'd leave his life above ground behind. But Kate was in his mind again, the way she'd hummed as she stepped from rung to rung, quiet notes of defiance against her fear of small, dark spaces.

At the bottom of the chamber, the brightness above was like a skylight in a crypt.

He moved down a side passage, darkness enclosing him. The air was cold on his hands and face. He stopped for a moment and extinguished his headlamp. Blackness seeped into his pores. His mind cleared. He pictured the route, silently mapping it, giving himself the talk. *Arms in front, be calm, breathe.*

He flicked the lamp back on and continued. The ceiling grew lower and the walls pressed towards him. Earthy dankness was all around. Rock rubbed one shoulder then the other.

At first he hunched, then he was forced to crawl. As he approached the Cement Bags section, he removed his backpack and slung himself on his belly. Usually this long tunnel was dusty, but today the floor was moist. It was easier without the powdery dirt flying up into his face, and he scrunched along swiftly on his elbows, repeatedly pushing his bag ahead. In under a minute he was through.

It was good to get upright for a while, passing through gaps between rock faces and crossing small chambers. Turning a corner, he arrived at the Hairy Traverse and dropped to his stomach.

Holding the chain, he began to inch up the rocky slope, sliding his backpack in front with one hand. He kept his head low. Whenever he looked to the right, his light beam swung out into nothing, into the dark mouth of the canyon. As he passed across, he measured each movement.

On the other side, he stood and moved on, winding deeper towards Hogans Hole. He kept a regular pace, his breathing even. The scrape of his boots echoed off the walls.

He was mentally preparing for the last challenge – the Log Jam – when he noticed the cave walls were shining wet. As he advanced, the passageway grew boggy. The roof lowered and he was forced to crawl through puddles. He shivered, his pant legs soaked. He'd checked the forecast this morning – there'd been nothing.

He paused on hands and knees, Kate's voice in his head. *Why do you go alone? Why can't you join a group like everyone else?*

Lincoln kept crawling. The rock ground his knees through the wet fabric and he wished he'd worn knee pads. But he was alright. He knew what he was doing. His father had told him since he was eight or nine to deal with things himself, and with his mother long gone – off in Sydney with some bloke – he'd had no choice.

Water sparkled on the walls wherever he looked but he was glad there were no more puddles. Then he rounded the corner to the Log Jam and saw the stretch of water, widening as the tunnel narrowed and dipped. It was shallow at first, but when he shone his headlamp further, water reached to the roof. He recalled the radar image from that morning, not a blot on the feed.

The air rose high in his lungs. This was a bad place to stop, and it might be flooded now back at the Cement Bags. He would go through the squeeze, and emerge in Hogans Hole where he could climb above the water, wait out the storm.

His arms trembled but he crawled on, until his only option was to wriggle like a snake in the muck. His hands were numb.

At the edge of the puddle he stopped and removed his bag,

the sounds of his own movements filling his ears. He began the breathe-up, closing his eyes, exhaling longer than his inhales. His heartbeat slowed.

Pushing the backpack ahead, he shunted forward. The water was an icy shock to his chin, then it was all around, then over him. He shoved the bag through, even as his shoulders touched the sides of the Log Jam.

Though it had been only seconds under water, his lungs already twitched, itching to breathe. He couldn't understand; usually he was sure and controlled in traps like this. Fear clawed at his brain. He kicked in the mud to find a foothold. His elbows sloshed, searching for traction. He slid a few centimetres, then stopped. The cave gripped him in its teeth.

It was always tight, but not like this. The water had swollen his clothes. The urge to inhale was unbearable, coming in powerful waves.

He forced himself to release the last of his air, a final, yielding sigh. His diaphragm jolted. Pinpricks of light danced beneath his eyelids.

He humped forward, a big push and a strong pull with his arms. This time a shoulder popped through, but he was still under water and his ribs bucked in desperation. He scrabbled until he freed his other shoulder, his chest screaming for air, then dragged himself a few more feet. His head broke the surface and he gasped like a dying man. He'd made it to the wide passage leading to Hogans Hole.

Lincoln knelt in the muck, panting and coughing. Water flowed down the walls and dripped onto his neck. Huge shudders passed through his body.

He closed his eyes, head hung low. *Kate. Kate, I'm sorry.*

Finally, the coughing eased and Lincoln pulled his bag from the water. There was a constant rushing sound. He stood on shaky legs.

The light of Hogans Hole spilled down the passage, but as he got close he saw it was oddly dim. Stormy skies loomed above. The water in the chamber was knee high, sloshing on his legs. The walls were too steep for him to exit; he'd planned to return via Fossil Cave.

Lincoln clambered onto boulders, kept going until he reached the highest point, well above the water, tucked away from the downpour.

He sat on the smooth boulder, his head filled with the clean smell of rain. He would find Kate, tell her he'd made a terrible mistake. He'd ask her to forgive him. He prayed she would take him back.

Rain teemed into Hogans Hole. The water inched upwards, lapping at the rocks.

AFTERSHOCK

As MAIA WALKS THROUGH THE wide foyer, the ground shimmies. She stops, her feet apart, and others do the same – everyone playing statues on this cold Tuesday afternoon. Then the movement is gone, and people continue in the hospital. Maia hurries to the Riverside Building, rushing to the lift before the doors close. Her blouse is damp against her skin. She used to be so casual with tremors, but now the slightest vibration sends her heart rate through the roof.

All across the city there are gaps where buildings crumbled or were pulled down after the earthquake. Cathedral Square is still closed, and Christchurch Cathedral is fenced off, the spire just a stump. High Street, where Maia's mother worked, is deserted even four years on – just rubbly parking lots and the wind blowing rubbish in the gutters. Sometimes Maia drives by, staring, her eyeballs so dry they hurt.

By the time the lift slows at the fourth floor, Maia's pulse is steady. She touches the ring hanging warm on her chest. As the lift opens, she feels the gaze of other nurses on her back. She's heard their comments before – *Oh God, oncology?*

So depressing. Squaring her shoulders, she steps out.

Down past reception, the whiteboard list shows Gertrude McLaren is still in Bed 11 and Maia smiles.

After staff handover, Sandra consults the patient list, serious as always in her team leader role. 'Maia, you okay to take bays five and six?'

'Sure, no problem.' Maia knows she's getting off easily. Bay 5 has only two beds and one of them is vacant.

The staff rapidly disperse. Buzzers are going, medications are due and any minute now visitors will arrive and ask for vases, pillows, biscuits and other things that don't really help the patients but make the visitors feel better. Maia heads down towards Bay 6, where Emily has pressed the call button.

Halfway there, a rumbling travels through the floor. Even once it passes, Maia stands rigid, deafened by the whoosh of her heart. Seconds pass. She walks on.

In Bay 6, she speaks softly to Emily, and fetches a wafer for the young woman's nausea. The others in the bay are asleep, and Maia is grateful. She thinks of her sister's prodding lately – 'We could move, go somewhere without quakes. Like Australia?' But she's always lived in Christchurch, all her whānau is here. The city reminds her of a fickle boyfriend – the one you plan to leave but then they swear undying love, promise to do better, and somehow you stay.

The blinds are closed in Bay 5, and she squints to see in the gloom. One bed is made up with tight, clean linen, and the other bed holds Gertrude, her snowy head indenting the pillow. It's not until Maia is beside the old lady that she sees her eyes are cracked open.

'Hi, Gertie! I thought you were asleep.'

The old lady slow-blinks. 'I'm awake. Thinking.'

Maia rests her arms on the side rail of the bed. At handover she heard how Gertie had been confused last night, struggling up to 'catch a bus home'.

'Can I get you anything?'

Gertrude shakes her head. Her lips are mauve and her face is powder-white.

'Do you have any pain?' Maia's been nursing seven years, knows patients like Gertie will suffer in silence, not wanting to be a bother.

Again, Gertrude shakes her head.

'Okay. I'll bring the phone later. When your son calls.'

The old lady's face lights up. 'Oh no.' Her voice is hoarse and she coughs, tries again. 'No call today. He's coming … to visit!' She lifts a hand above the sheet, folding thin bony fingers over the edge. 'You'll get to meet … my Tony. My boy.'

Maia makes herself smile. 'Sounds good!' Her cheeks are stiff. Gertie's son, her only child, hasn't visited once, despite the fact he lives in Christchurch. They've all discussed it, the whole team.

Gertrude closes her eyes, her lips still turned up at the corners. 'You'll like him.'

Maia busies herself, tidying Gertrude's bedside table, and moving her plastic mug closer. 'Want any water before I go?'

'No thank you … darling.'

'Okay then. See you in a bit.'

~

Maia sneaks the last bite of a Chocolate Fish, chewing sweet marshmallow as she writes up patient notes. It's almost eight o'clock and the ward is settling for the night. The main lights in each bay have been switched off, and just the small lights are on above the beds. Some of the sicker patients have their lights off. Most of the visitors are gone.

Often at this time, a brief lull in the late shift, Maia thinks of her mother. She still has the ridiculous conviction that her mother is close by, just a suburb away, if only she could find her.

As she closes the chart, she remembers Gertie's hoped-for visitor, the son who never arrived. Maia bins the wrapper and slots the charts back. She passes Bay 6, where televisions flicker and Emily is reading *The Kite Runner*. In her bed near the window, Rani is already snoring.

Gertrude's room is shadowy. Her above-bed light is off, but the ensuite door is open, and a shaft of light falls across the bed. The old lady lies on her back, cheekbones shiny where the skin is pulled tight. It will be two or three days, no more.

The bedsheet is pushed down and uneven at Gertie's hips. Maia lifts the white fabric until it billows, then lets it float to her patient's chest. She is about to leave when she sees the dark figure near the window, on the far side of the vacant bed.

'Geez, you scared me.' Her eyes trace the tall, broad outline – a man.

'Sorry. Didn't want to disturb you.' He moves into the low light near Gertie's bed. His features become defined – strong nose, big chin, thick greying hair. 'I was about to go. She's sleeping, anyway.'

The old lady's eyes are closed, her mouth slightly open. The man watches her, his face blank as cardboard.

Maia steps into the hallway, motioning him to follow. 'Are you her son?'

He crosses his arms, drops his gaze to his boots. 'Yeah. Tony. How's she doing?'

'Bit late to be asking now.'

These past few years, her anger sits just below the surface. Being polite to arseholes takes all her self-control, and sometimes a few barbed words slip through.

Tony lifts his big head, and he looks like he's been slapped.

Maia feels a spike of regret. Then she thinks of Gertie alone, day after day. 'She's not eating, and today she stopped drinking. It won't be long now. Two days, maybe three.'

Tony nods and runs a hand across his forehead. 'Right. Two days. Okay.' He trudges towards the ward entrance, then turns. 'Thank you, nurse.'

Maia doesn't reply.

She knows what Sandra would say. That she's got too close to Gertie, that she hasn't kept a 'professional boundary'. It's hard to stay detached, though. She's with each patient through the worst time of their life. Sometimes until the end.

Tony slumps away. He looks older from behind as he heads to the lifts. She's watching him jab at the button when a thundering sound begins, like heavy machinery rolling down the hall. This time the whole ward gently shakes. A linen cupboard swings open and a towel falls out. Maia clutches a sink, her legs weak.

Within a few seconds, the ward is still.

Tony rushes back. 'That was a decent one. Had to be a five.' He's puffing. 'I hope there's nothing bigger coming.'

Maia clasps her hands to hide her agitation. 'I don't know. Listen, I've got patients to check.' Up and down the corridor, nurses are heading into rooms.

Maia ducks back into Gertie's room, switching on the light. Everything is in order. The old lady stirs, her focus on something past Maia. 'Tony. My Tony.' Her eyes brim with tears.

Tony stands in the doorway, arms dangling at his sides. He doesn't move; it's like his shoes are glued to the floor. Maia wants to bark at him to snap out of it, to just go to his mother, but she's had two warnings already for speaking sharply to relatives. She slips past the man without saying a word. She'll describe her restraint to the counsellor on Thursday.

In Bay 6, some of Emily's toiletries have fallen from her cupboard, and she's crying softly. Her book lies splayed on her bedside table. 'Emily, you okay?' Maia flicks on the main light. The others are awake too, but nothing else is out of place.

'Yes.' Emily's reply is barely audible.

'Everyone else alright?'

The others murmur that they're fine, but Emily's eyes are glazed.

'You're feeling queasy, aren't you?'

The girl nods, the veins showing green beside her mouth.

'I'll get you something. Won't be long.'

~

It's half an hour before Maia returns to Gertie. Emily needed medication and a sick bag. Rani wanted heat packs and painkillers. After all that, Hazel said she'd never get to sleep and asked for a tablet.

Gertie's room is quiet, but when Maia leans closer she sees a wet line from Gertie's eye to her ear. The old lady's breathing catches as it ebbs and flows.

Maia bends to speak softly near the small, dishevelled head. 'Gertie, what's wrong?'

Gertie's lips quiver. 'He's not … coming back.'

Maia's legs are aching – it's been a long shift and she still has an hour to go. 'You mean Tony? Tony's not coming back?'

'He said … he was here … to say goodbye.' Gertie turns away, her mouth working and twisting. She pauses, then looks back at Maia. 'It's okay. He's a good boy.' Her lips are so dry they have splits in several places. 'I wasn't always … the best mother.'

'Well, who is? No one's perfect.' Maia touches Gertie's thin, gnarled hand. She thinks of her mother's hands, how they'd been starting to wrinkle, turning velvety soft.

Maia runs a thumb across Gertie's wrist, and stays bending there. Gertie's eyes drift closed.

~

It is almost eleven when Maia finally walks out the main doors. Her sister messaged that she was leaving work, although sometimes that means she just hopes to leave. Maia flops on a bench along the wall and pulls out her Marlboros. She's cutting down, she's going to quit soon, but a smoke after work helps her unwind.

As she turns her back against the breeze, she sees someone on the opposite bench. A tiny orange glow appears and disappears. The man's shag of hair is just visible in the dim light. She takes a long pull on her cigarette, grinds it out and strides over.

'Your mum was crying when you left.' She can't go on, she's too choked-up.

Tony stamps his cigarette beneath his boot. 'You don't know. You don't fucking know.' He gazes across the road, into the darkness of Hagley Park.

When he speaks again, he sounds like he's shivering. 'It started when I was maybe three or four.'

Goosebumps rise up on Maia's arms.

'I'd be eating my toast at the kitchen table and something would set her off.' Tony grips his fist. 'Anything. Maybe I was spilling crumbs, or I was kicking the table leg, not knowing. She would grab my arm and pull me down the hall.'

He studies his boots. 'And I knew what was coming. I'd cry, and grab at doorways and I'd say, "No, please no, Mum, I'll be good."'

Maia wishes her sister would show up, prays that Anika has locked the café, driven off and is about to arrive. But Tony continues.

'When she got puffed, or when the handle broke, she'd shut me in the wardrobe and tie it closed.'

Maia is chilled to the core. Not her Gertie.

'I hated that the most.' Tony's voice is flat. 'It was so bloody dark.'

A car pulls to the kerb, and a young man from the back seat helps the pregnant passenger out, his arm under hers, before the car moves away.

The wind stirs the trees across the road.

'Maybe she couldn't cope, when you were little? Had depression or something?' Even as she says it, Maia knows it is wrong to make excuses.

Tony shrugs. 'I've given up trying to figure it out.'

'God.' Maia doesn't know what to say. Her childhood wasn't easy – not much money, her mum always working, her dad just a face in a photo. She and Anika sometimes screamed and fought, and then her mum would yell. But she remembers lots of laughing too.

She feels sick to think what Gertie did.

Maia eases down onto Tony's bench.

He pulls out his cigarettes, stares at the pack, then returns it to his jacket. 'After a while, someone told child services. We were in government housing – an apartment – so I guess a neighbour heard. A social worker started visiting. I went to school. It was better.'

'So, she was kind, after that?'

Tony sighs. 'Look, she stopped the worst of it. And I left home when I was fourteen.'

They sit in silence. The wind picks up and the trees fling their branches side to side. Leaves twirl beneath the streetlights.

The bright blue hatchback pulls up sharply. Anika is in the driver's seat, her smile uncertain. Maia gives her a wave.

'I'm sorry. I had no idea.' She meets Tony's eyes.

Tony pulls his collar up, gives a sad shrug. 'She seems like a nice old lady, right?'

Maia wonders if he's heard this many times, people telling him to treat his mother better. She pictures the fine white hair on Gertie's pillow, hears the sweet quaver: *Hello, Maia!*

Maia is hollow inside, like when she drives past High Street.

'Every time I see her it messes with my head. My shrink finally told me to stay away.' Tony rubs his jaw. 'So I haven't seen her, not for ages. I just phone.' He gestures to Anika. 'You'd better get going.'

Maia stands. She can do this. 'She'll have the very best care, your mum.' Her mind jumps to her own mum. She had no one that day, when all the buildings came down.

Maia makes her voice confident and calm. 'We'll look after her, keep her comfortable. And at the very end, I'll be there.'

Tony's eyes glisten. His Adam's apple shifts in his throat.

She hurries to the car and gets in. Anika starts asking

questions, but Maia's thoughts are spinning like the leaves in Hagley Park.

She'll keep her promise. Tony's mother will be cared for with compassion. And when the final hours come, Maia will sit by her side.

She'll hold Gertie's hand so carefully and so gently, it will almost feel like love.

LAST GAME

IT WAS JUST AFTER SUNSET, one of those warm summer evenings that seem like they'll never end. We were running in a pack, little squirts to big kids, playing hide-and-seek. As dusk fell, Blake disappeared and returned with a flashlight.

'Guys! Let's play Ghost!'

Ghost in the Graveyard was our favourite game. We roamed between Blake's place and Mai Lee's, spanning four small wooden homes in the post-grad student housing. Not long ago we'd spook anywhere in the street, but a murder in our town had got our parents making rules.

'Last game,' Mai Lee's mother called.

The adults sat on the sidewalk in folding chairs, drinking wine and chatting, their cigarettes like fireflies. Jenny's mom was bleary-eyed, slumped in her seat. Blake's dad stroked his moustache, staring at the long, tanned legs of another mom as she passed around prunes wrapped in bacon. My dad rambled on about Nixon, gesturing with his empty glass. Whenever he saw me, he called out, 'Susan! Sweetheart! Having a good time?' Mostly I pretended not to hear him. He was trying hard to be both mom and dad, but sometimes he was just a pain.

I was a scrawny girl with buck teeth and a chin like a rat. I had all the wrong clothes and I talked too much. Since I'd turned eleven, though, things were looking up. A few older kids had left the neighbourhood gang and I'd snuck in from the edges.

We started out at Mai Lee's place. It was her turn to be the ghost, and she clowned around, making claws with her hands and widening her eyes. We all sniggered but the truth was, she was freaking me out. Little Jenny edged close, chewing the collar of her dress. I held Dad's new Maglite® in a damp grip.

There were a lot of us that night – maybe fifteen or so. Just like always, we turned to face the door and Mai Lee ran away. We started counting, 'One o'clock, two o'clock.' We counted slow and heavy, to give the ghost a chance to hide, and the sound of our chanting sent chills down my spine. Right after 'eleven o'clock' we screamed, 'Midnight!' and switched on our flashlights.

'Spread out, spread out, guys!' Blake was starting eighth grade in the fall, and he bossed us all around. I didn't mind. He had black hair and red lips; I hoped to marry him one day.

Lights bobbed through the night as the others moved away, most of them in pairs. I looked around for Jenny, but she was holding another girl's hand. I shivered, wishing I'd worn more than a tube top and shorts.

I wandered into Mai Lee's backyard, poking my light into the doghouse. Nothing. The swings dangled, empty. No grinning girl crouched behind the daisies.

As I headed out towards the street, a movement near the fence caught my attention. A boy about my height stood in the glare of my beam, one hand raised to shield his eyes. He held an unlit flashlight. His mouth tucked down at the corners, as if he was about to cry.

Quickly I aimed the Maglite® on my dirty bare feet. 'You new here?' I stayed cool and calm.

'Yep.'

'Your battery dead?'

'Uh-huh.'

'You can share mine,' I said. 'We'll find her together.'

'Okay,' he said from somewhere a little closer. His feet appeared in the bright circle. 'My name's Clem.'

'I'm Susan. Let's go this way.' I pointed to the road and we walked together.

Out on the kerb, it was strangely quiet. The other kids must have found Mai Lee, and switched off their lights. Now they were ghosts too.

I sighed. 'Looks like it's just us.'

Under the streetlamp I could see Clem better. His cheeks were smooth, and white-blond hair fell across his eyes.

'Let's head to Jenny's,' I said. 'She has a garden shed. I bet they're in there.'

His shadowed gaze was steady. 'Okay then.'

I led the way down the gravel path, our feet crunching in the silence. A swift shape flapped past us and I drew back, bumping into Clem with a skittering laugh.

'It's a snowy owl,' he whispered, pointing. The bird's white face reflected dimly from a nearby tree.

'Really?' I asked, squinting.

'Yeah. They live up north, in the Arctic. But every few years they come down to Oregon.' He was motionless, studying the owl. 'And no one knows why.'

My shoulders brushed his chest and I was dizzy with his nearness. We breathed together in the dark.

A shout came from somewhere close, and I remembered the game.

'We better keep going.'

'Alright.' His soft voice gave me goosebumps.

We walked towards the shed, slower and slower. I stopped and touched his arm. 'If they're in there, I'll race you back and the loser is up. Okay?'

'Sure,' Clem said.

I pulled the shed door open, iron scraping on concrete. The smell of grass and oil drifted out. My light strobed across lawnmowers and furniture. Down one side ran a workbench with glass jars along the wall and tools hanging above. There were spiderwebs draped everywhere, undisturbed.

'They're not here.' I was swept with a familiar shame.

I turned to Clem but he was gone. The only sound was the shushing of trees, shifting in the breeze. I spun back to the shed, then around to the yard. I was alone. He'd left me too.

Last month's TV news echoed in my mind, the newsreader weirdly cheerful: *The body was found in a storm drain. Police are yet to detain a suspect.*

I glanced at the trees near the fence line. Their branches were wild now, thrashing like arms. The shushing was louder. And right in the corner of the yard was a tall shape. A man, just standing there.

'Mr Bukowski?' My knees were like Jell-O. 'Is that you?'

There was no reply. The man waited, arms wide as if ready to grab me.

The moon slid from behind a cloud and the sky brightened.

I was exposed, a floodlit target. I sprinted for the street, racing for my life.

~

They must have heard me coming. The adults were silent and my dad had risen from his chair. 'What's up, Suse?'

I bent to my knees, panting so hard I could barely speak. 'A man. In the yard. Jenny's place.'

Dad frowned. 'A man? What do you mean? Did someone chase you?' He peered behind me, reaching to draw me close.

'No.' I glanced around. Already my fear was receding, and I felt foolish. 'No, he just stood there, watching.' I nestled into my father.

Dad sat down and pulled me onto his lap, something he hadn't done since my mom left. 'You know what? I bet it was their scarecrow.' A few parents murmured in agreement, chuckling and shifting in their chairs, the moonlight catching on their teeth.

I hung my head. 'Oh yeah. I forgot about the scarecrow.'

'Don't worry, bug. It would have freaked me out too.' My father tucked my tangled hair behind my ears. I leant back against him, gazing at the star-studded sky.

After a while I sat up. My pulse was slow again.

'Going to watch the Disney movie?' Dad kissed my temple. 'They're all at Mai Lee's.'

The sinking feeling returned. Why hadn't someone come to find me?

'Okay.' I wandered off in the dark.

~

Mai Lee's house smelt different, but in a good way. It smelt of meat and rice and cabbage. Her dad was a great cook. I inhaled deeply as I came through the open door and into the living room.

All the lights were off, and the kids' faces were blue in the glow of the TV. On-screen, Goofy tried over and over to climb onto a horse. I scanned the room. Everyone stayed glued to the movie.

I waved a hand in front of me. 'Hey, guys. Where's Clem?'

A few stares flicked my way, but only Blake answered. 'Who's Clem?'

I yanked my top higher beneath my arms. 'You know. The new kid. His flashlight wasn't working.'

Blake shook his head, eyes on the television. 'Nup. Dunno any Clem.'

I chewed my lip. 'He had blond hair. This tall.' I flattened my hand just above my head.

The kids sat crammed together on the couch and on the floor. Jenny curled on the rug, fast asleep. No one replied.

I hated cartoons, and anyway I'd seen that Goofy movie. I slouched into the kitchen where a plate of chocolate chip cookies sat on the benchtop, covered in Saran Wrap. Lifting the edge, I pulled out a cookie and flopped at the table, thinking about the new boy, wondering why he'd run away. When I finished, I brushed the crumbs off the newspaper in front of me. A photo of Clem emerged. I leant closer, excited to see his face. Reading the words, I froze.

Police have now revealed the victim's identity as Clem Hatcher, aged twelve years, of College Hill, Eugene (picture at left).

The cookie was a sickly paste in my mouth.

~

'Come on, Suse.' I heard my dad among the rumble of adult voices on Mai Lee's porch. 'Time to go.'

I crawled out from under the table, wiping my eyes. The other kids were stumbling away and someone turned the TV off. I followed the trail of children out the door and Dad and I headed home. He had a camp chair under one arm and a box of Graham Crackers in the other.

'Was it a good movie?'

I gazed at his smiling face, creased and kind in the shadows. He walked with an easy lope, the way he always did after a few glasses of wine.

'Yeah. It was good.'

He ruffled my hair. 'And no more phantoms came after you?'

I forced a laugh. 'Nah.' We were nearly home now.

He switched the crackers to the other side and I took his hand. It was big and warm. I paced my steps in time with his.

'You know that kid who got killed?'

He looked down at me. 'The boy?'

'Clem,' I said. I pictured Clem's serious expression, his flop of blond hair.

'Was that his name?' My father leant the chair against our house and opened the front door.

'Yeah.' I looked back into the night, rubbing my arms. 'His name is Clem.'

HAPPY HOUR

Symphonies 25–43, Mozart

Colin pressed the button on the mixing desk, leaning closer to the microphone.

'And that, folks, is that. I'll be signing off to get some shut-eye.' He unbuttoned his shirt, thinking of his soft bed, just down the hall. 'For those staying up, I've got a real treat for you. Nineteen Mozart symphonies. A Mozart marathon, if you will.' He chuckled. 'For everyone else, goodnight, sleep tight.'

He turned the microphone off and stood, shrugging out of his shirt. It was a fancy one, blue with purple paisley inside the cuffs. His daughter had given it to him last birthday, saying, 'Perfect for picking up chicks, Dad.' But he wasn't interested in any of that.

In the bedroom, he hung his shirt on the chair and tapped his tablet awake, clicking on the forecast for Katoomba.

Max 19. Sunny morning. Winds 30–50 km/h. High (80%) chance of heavy rain later in the day.

Colin closed the tablet, uneasy. He'd never minded squally weather, but lately it bothered him. Many things worried him that never did before. He supposed it was to do with missing Elaine.

He slipped off his shoes and stepped out of his trousers, folding them over the seat of the chair. Pulling the doona back, he slid into bed.

The clock read 22:05, so at least he was on schedule. The routine worked well – dinner during one piece of music, feeding the cat and doing his stretches in another. As the final piece played, he'd use the toilet and brush his teeth. He didn't like to leave his listeners too long. Once, when he'd had a sudden gastric attack and the Peer Gynt suites had finished before he could return, Pat from Blackheath had called, terribly worried. The silence had been awful, she'd said.

Colin switched off the lamp and lay on his back. A branch tapped at the window, the lilly pilly he'd been meaning to trim. He rested his hands on his bony chest, the muted thumping of his heart beneath his fingers. The constancy of the muscle always amazed him.

Dear Lord, he prayed, *please care for Elaine. Keep her safe until I'm with her again.*

It was a prayer he'd said each evening while his wife was in hospital, and then when she was in palliative care. Four years later, he couldn't seem to break the habit.

Colin raised his fingers to his lips. He kissed them, then spread his hands wide in the dark. 'Goodnight, sweetheart,' he said.

~

Symphony No. 43, Mozart / String Quartet No. 14, Beethoven
Colin woke to the branch hitting the glass, a repeating *thwack*. Something went skittering along the terrace – the plastic watering can, he guessed. The clock read 05:49, one minute before the alarm.

In the kitchen, he filled the kettle. As he waited for it to boil, the shadows in the yard disappeared, trees and bushes revealing themselves, tossing in the wind. He'd be alright inside, a warm cuppa in hand, feet cosy in his slippers. He had a big day planned – Debussy, Chopin, a little Rachmaninoff. While each was playing he'd prepare a new overnight playlist, provisionally titled *Telemann Treasures*.

The phone rang and he frowned, glancing at the microwave clock. 05:54. He had to be on air in six minutes. His hand hovered then retreated. Finally, he lifted the mobile.

'Colin Peelgrane speaking.'

'Dad, it's me. Didn't you see the number?'

'Oh hello, love! You know I never look at that.'

'Anyway, want to have lunch?' Tara sounded unusually cheery. 'I've got a client in Penrith. We could meet in Hazelbrook.'

Colin walked to his studio, once the spare bedroom.

He'd talked about starting a station for years, and when she was near the end, Elaine had made him promise to do it. Twelve months after she died, he'd moved the ironing board, exercise bike and boxes of CDs into the lounge. The studio had grey foam soundproofing on every wall, and was equipped with headphones, microphone, CD stack and mixing board. He'd set it all up with his friend Angelo, another retired electrician.

'Ah, let me see ...' Colin ran his finger down his scheduled programming.

Tara was suddenly abrupt. 'You're not going to say you can't, are you? That you haven't got time?' She paused, then spoke gently. 'If it's the drive, I'll come to you.'

A dull headache was beginning at his temples. 'No, no, Hazelbrook is fine.' It was twenty minutes' drive, he could manage. He drew a line through a Debussy piece and scrawled

Das Rhinegold. The Wagner opera would be perfect – two hours forty minutes.

'What time? Where?'

Tara gave him details – she researched these things, never ate out without checking reviews – as he watched the minutes tick towards six o'clock.

'Okay, love, see you then.' He rushed to the desk, pulling on headphones, speaking in his smoothest, deepest voice. 'Good morning, friends! I hope you're starting your day well, perhaps with a nice strong coffee or a piping hot tea.' He thought longingly of the teapot on the bench, waiting for scalding water.

'First up, I'll be taking requests for Happy Hour, the usual five till six slot. If you'd like one of your favourites, give me a call. Same number – 7010 4238.' He inched up the volume on the next piece. 'And now, here's Beethoven's String Quartet No. 14. This sublime piece in C-sharp minor was played for Franz Schubert on his deathbed, as his final musical request.'

Colin sat listening as the two violins sang back and forth, then in harmony. The viola moaned, and the cello rumbled. The melody rose, and rose again, like a slow ascent to heaven.

~

Das Rhinegold, Wagner

The car wouldn't steer straight, blown towards the verge. Colin adjusted his course, knuckles aching from the effort. He didn't mind short trips to the nursery or to book club, and he was happy to pop out to the supermarket, where he'd almost always see someone he knew. But even in fine conditions, longer drives set his teeth on edge. It was cold for January, and Colin was glad he'd worn his Kathmandu jacket.

Leaves lay scattered across the bitumen, and the occasional branch caused him to veer into the other lane. The sky was a clear, cool blue.

He was relieved to arrive in Hazelbrook, and find the café. Tara was already seated, menus and water on the table. She stood to hug him.

'Looking very outdoors-y, Dad,' she said.

Clearly he should have worn something better. A tasteful woollen jumper, perhaps.

He smiled. 'Lovely to see you, Tara.'

They both chose open sandwiches, and Tara ordered at the counter.

'So, Dad.' His daughter settled back in her seat, pulling a glossy brochure from her bag. There were several grey-haired people on the cover, all with oddly smooth faces. 'Angus and I were talking ...' She stopped, spreading her hands across the shiny surface. She wasn't meeting Colin's eye. 'You know, you're seventy-five this year, and you're on your own.'

'Yes.' He didn't like where this was going. His kids were conspiring.

Tara opened the booklet and passed it across. 'What do you think?'

Colin placed the brochure on the table. He picked up his reading glasses, and with infinite care, slid them behind his ears, adjusting their position on the bridge of his nose. He peered at the text. Words jumped out at him: *Peace of mind. 24-hour nurse. Craft days.*

The place was called Evergreen, and it was a suburb away from Tara and her family.

Tara's expression flicked between pride and trepidation.

Just as slowly as he'd donned his glasses, Colin removed them, folding in each arm.

'This isn't for me. I have the station, my friends, the garden. I don't want mush on a tray, old people dribbling around me.'

His daughter sat back in her chair. 'Dad! That's not what it's like. You'd be in your own flat, with a bedroom, bathroom and living space.'

Colin's head ached, the tight band returning. He'd visited a friend once, in such a flat. Its tiny dimensions had shocked him, and he'd smelt an unpleasant bathroom odour from the small round table where they'd sipped their tea.

'Tara, no. That's not what I want.'

His daughter's face reminded him of when she was a child, the same stubborn set of her features. They sat in silence until the waiter swooped in with their meals.

~

Four Seasons, Vivaldi

Colin plonked himself in the swivel chair. He was making his extended Telemann mix, and it was almost done, despite the two hours lost over lunch. Outside it was blustery, and clouds had gathered in the west. There was dampness in the air.

His mind wandered back to the conversation with Tara. She'd really gone to town, trying to convince him. It wasn't fair, the way she'd brought up his knee replacement last year, and the fact he didn't drive much anymore. She'd even talked about the house and yard, how there were so many trees and hedges. He hadn't bothered to mention his neighbour's son Lucas, who mowed and trimmed for a very reasonable fee. She'd made up her mind.

Colin faded out one concerto and raised the volume on the next. This would be an exciting playlist. Marvin from Wentworth Falls might ring tomorrow morning, say how much he'd liked it. Marvin had some kind of back complaint and couldn't sleep at night. He said listening to *Classic Calm* eased his pain. And dear old Lacey from Leura might call up early to compliment the list. She'd once told Colin that any piece by Telemann cheered her right up for the rest of the day.

At 15:12, Colin went in search of a snack. The kitchen was gloomy, and the camellias near the back fence thrashed like fretful children.

Just as Colin reached into the pantry, there was an almighty crack. He flinched, and as he spun around, a huge limb of blue gum thundered to the lawn. The branch was as wide as a man's body, large enough to kill. He imagined the strike of it against his skull.

At the window, he could see the raw, splintered wound where the tree had lost its arm. Rain spotted the glass and he edged away. The branch would be well beyond Lucas; someone would need to chainsaw the wood and remove it. A helpless feeling billowed inside him.

~

Brandenburg Concertos 1–6, Bach
By 17:03, the house was almost dark and rain fell in fits and starts. Colin kept shifting in his studio chair. He was playing the Brandenburg Concertos, which Elaine had once described as 'like angels having a party'. But something felt wrong. It wasn't just the weather, or the giant branch, or the tense talk he'd had with Tara over lunch. Lacey hadn't called.

It was an unspoken agreement. Every afternoon, Lacey called on the dot of four. She'd ask in her thin, silvery voice, all light and casual, if he had a full list for his Happy Hour. She made it sound like he'd be doing her a favour, taking her request. The truth was, *Classic Calm* had a loyal but small following. At least half the time, when Lacey called, he'd received no Happy Hour suggestions.

'Well, if you can squeeze it in, how about some Handel?' she might say. She was never too specific, careful not to cause inconvenience.

'Oh, I reckon I can dig something up,' he'd reply. And a feeling would spread through him, not happiness exactly but a gladness.

Today, the phone was silent.

Colin spun the chair sideways, stretching his legs. He tried to think what he knew about Lacey. They never talked for long, just a minute or two. He thought from her voice that she was much older than him, perhaps in her nineties. She'd mentioned a retired son in Sydney, and once she'd referred to gardening with her walker. 'Winston the Walker', she'd called it. But Colin didn't even know her last name.

The phone line on the mixing board stayed unlit. Colin clicked his pen on and off. The wind surged and eased, great raging gusts. His mobile rang and he jumped, but it was that same nuisance number, the one that always told him his computer needed fixing. He ignored it.

Lacey was fine, he told himself. She'd likely forgotten him for once. But the pit of his stomach told him no, that wasn't it. He picked up the phone, pressed three zeros, then didn't make the call. It wasn't an emergency, or if it was, he had no proof.

A memory unfurled like a flower. Lacey lived beside a walking track, some kind of bird name; it was on the tip of his tongue. *The Lyrebird Track.* One afternoon, she'd said she was off for a walk, lamenting she could no longer manage the trail.

He checked Google Maps and found her street in less than a minute.

Daylight had vanished. The rain was heavier, angry now. The idea of driving in this weather made him feel physically ill.

He hated the way fear had expanded in his life – that was partly why he'd been so cranky with Tara. Some of the things she'd been saying were right. When he was younger, he'd been confident and bold. He'd clambered around in lift shafts for work. He'd protested against the Vietnam War, been arrested twice. In the '86 floods, back in Sydney, he'd carried Tara and Angus through rising waters, a child in each arm, unafraid.

He pocketed his phone and keys, strode to the front door and grabbed his rain jacket from the hat stand. Even on the verandah, he was spattered with water as he hurried to the carport.

He drove down the street, his back rigid. The headlights seemed unnaturally weak and Colin flicked on high beam. The windscreen wipers made whining, frenzied arcs. No one else was out. It was only when he turned onto the Great Western Highway that he passed another vehicle. The car shuddered and Colin drove at fifty.

He trundled into Leura, taking slow turns right and left until he stopped at the end of Spencer Road. His high beam lit up the sign to the track. He swung carefully around, parking outside the smallest of the two houses at the end of the road.

As soon as Colin left the car, the breath was dragged from his body and rain smacked him in the face. He pulled up the hood of

215

his jacket and headed for the cottage. But before he reached the door, he spotted a swing set up the side, then almost tripped over a scooter, abandoned on the driveway.

Colin retraced his steps. Water dripped from his nose and flooded his eyes. He crossed the road and made his way towards the larger house, staggering with the wind. The porch light was on, but he could see no other lights as he passed through the gate. He pictured intruders, wearing black and wielding knives. He stopped, breathing fast.

Standing on the front path, Colin began to hear something, a faint piping like a bird, or a high note from a flute. It took a moment before he realised it was a word, flung with the wind. 'Hello?' it said. 'Hello?'

Colin pulled out his phone, hands shaking, and switched on the torch. His socks squelched in his shoes as he rounded the front garden bed, turning the corner.

A dark figure lay beside a walker frame. He sucked in air.

'Lacey? Is that you?'

The figure moved a little, then cried out and lay still.

He knelt beside the lady, ignoring the protests of his knees. 'It's Colin, from *Classic Calm*, you know, the station?'

She lay on her back. One shoe had fallen off.

'Oh.' Her reply came like a whisper, just a puff of air. 'Hello, Colin.' She showed no surprise.

'I'll get some help,' Colin said. He sat back on his heels and stabbed at his mobile. It rang for what felt like ages before someone picked up and took details.

'They want to know your name and age,' he shouted above the wind.

'Lacey Halland. I'm ninety-three.'

Colin relayed this and pocketed his phone.

'I'm going to cover you, alright?' He eased the jacket from his shoulders, and spread it across Lacey, shielding her tiny body up to her chin. He sat beside her, water seeping into the backside of his pants and rain slowly soaking his clothes.

'They'll be here soon,' he said.

Lacey didn't respond. Colin found her hand, cold and fragile as porcelain. He burned with energy despite the chilling rain.

'I have cuttings in pots,' Lacey panted. 'I wanted to bring them inside.'

Colin patted her hand. 'No one can blame you for that.'

'I slipped. There were leaves.'

Colin listened for the ambulance, heard nothing but the rustling of trees. 'These things happen.'

The rain had almost stopped, dwindling to the finest drizzle. There was a tangy metallic scent to the air. Colin tried to think of something else to say. Lacey's hand was limp.

'Hey, Lacey?'

Her fingers flickered in his grasp. 'Yes?'

'Should I play something for you? Tomorrow, for Happy Hour? Your son could find the station online.'

Lacey squeezed his hand. 'Yes. Please.'

'What would you like?' He would find it, whatever she requested.

'Jesu, Joy of Man's Desiring.'

Colin swallowed. That piece always put him through the wringer. Depleted him then restored him.

He would play the Philadelphia Orchestra recording.

~

Jesu, Joy of Man's Desiring, Bach

Colin spoke softly into the mic. 'Good afternoon, listeners, whoever you are, wherever you are.' He felt stiff from last night, but incredibly alive. 'The first piece in Happy Hour goes out to Lacey. Get better soon, my friend.'

Lacey's son had phoned in on his mother's instructions. He'd sounded bemused, but had let Colin know Lacey was doing well. She had a fractured collarbone and a badly sprained ankle, but was out of hospital already.

Colin adjusted his headphones and slid the fader up on the mixing desk. 'So here it is. Jesu, Joy of Man's Desiring by Johann Sebastian Bach.' The music streamed into his ears – first the strings, in humble waves, then the oboe, soaring and saintly. He hoped Lacey was listening.

Closing his eyes, Colin sat back in the chair, hands clasped across his chest. The orchestra played on. His heart kept its own rhythm, strong and steady, like it might just beat forever.

CHRISTMAS
PARTY

'FOR GODSAKE, FRANK, WHAT'S THE RUSH?'

Her father didn't react, just pressed the doorbell. Lana and her mother picked their way up the dark, icy driveway.

'You just charge ahead. No thought for me!' Her mom wobbled along, elbows out, placing her feet with care.

Lana followed, boots skidding sideways with each step. Her breath billowed from her mouth and her lungs burned. Under the yellow porch light, her dad stood with arms crossed, his face like a wall. The door with its green and red wreath swung inwards.

'Hi, guys, come on in. Hi, Lana.' Mr Perron held the door wide and she hunched in after her parents.

'Hello, Mr Perron!' The greeting squeaked from her mouth and her cheeks flared hot.

Her teacher's husband closed the door, eyes crinkling above his beard. 'Good to see you.'

Lana smiled back at him, ignoring the pinch of her woollen dress. Lately she was wider, and all her clothes were tight. When she moved around, she bumped into things with her bottom and stomach. Her mother said it was puppy fat, that she was about to grow tall, but she knew it was plain old fat. The grade seven boys called her Lumpy Lana. She sucked in her belly as she passed her coat to Mr Perron.

'Yvette's still getting ready.' He nodded towards the hallway. 'I'll just put your things away. Head on through.'

Lana followed her parents to the living room, where candles flickered from the corners and a tinselled tree sat against one window. A bearskin rug lay on the brown shag carpet. Her mother perched on an armchair and her dad flopped onto a couch, one leg dangling. Music drifted from speakers, and her father sang along, a song about bridges and troubled waters.

Lana eyed the potato chips on the coffee table, wondering if her mother would hiss if she ate some. Before she could decide, her dad rose to his feet.

'Yvette! You're looking lovely.'

Mrs Perron hustled in, slim and gorgeous in a long paisley dress, eyelids sparkling like jewels. She hugged them all in a cloud of perfume. As her husband poured drinks, she laid a hand on Lana's shoulder, her breath fierce and winey.

'Let's get this party started!'

She swept to the record player and swapped records, dropping the needle with a shrieking scrape. A different song began, pulsing and beating. Lana knew this one – 'Night Fever' – it was always on the radio. The high voices crooned across the room. Mrs Perron began to dip her shoulders and shimmy her hips, her hair sliding over one eye. Lana backed away.

The doorbell rang, and more teachers arrived, bringing wine and eggnog and cheeseballs on pottery plates. They stood in clusters, all talking at once. Lana dived to snatch a fistful of chips, eating them so fast her chest hurt.

When she was younger, she'd crawl under tables at these parties, watching the shoes go past. Often she was the only child. She would fall asleep beneath the tablecloth then wake in the evening air as her father carried her to the car. Now she was too big to play under tables. She sat behind a sofa, knees bent close, picking at knobs of thread on her stockings.

'Well, I joke about it but I'm not too worried. She's always been a sturdy girl. Has the Baker appetite. And the Baker bottom!' Her mother laughed, and there was light laughter from the other teachers. Lana's eyes stung.

'She's fine how she is, though, don't you think?' Mr Perron piped up from a corner of the room. 'And smart as hell.'

'Well, sure. She's just a little chunky.'

'You know, Yvette says she's really bright.' His tone was mild.

'I know that.' Her mother's voice was brittle. 'I never said she wasn't.'

There was a brief hush before the kindy teacher leapt in, telling them how she'd got lost on her way.

~

Lana wriggled up from the beanbag. It was after midnight, but the party was still roaring. Music shook the walls and the house was overflowing. She ducked past teachers who might tug at her braids and make her waitress with trays of vol-au-vents. Her eyes were heavy, and she planned to curl up with the jackets on the guestroom bed. She wandered down the hall, scratching at the armpit of her dress.

The door was almost closed. She pushed, and it swung open. Dim light seeped across Mrs Perron and the gym teacher,

Mr Kondos, standing mashed together, mouths attached, arms grabbing and pulling.

Her father's laugh drifted down from the lounge room. She was afraid to move. Through the window, in the coloured glow of Christmas lights, snow fell like confetti. The teachers moaned and groped. Lana edged back, her feet soundless on the thick hall carpet. Mr Kondos opened an eye. She thudded away towards the music.

In the heat of the party, her father danced near the record player, the top buttons of his shirt undone, showing dark chest hair. He twisted and bumped with the kindergarten teacher, their faces gleaming. Now and then the music jumped as the needle skipped a groove.

Her mother sat enveloped by a couch, her green polyester pant legs emerging like droopy stalks. She sipped her drink, nodding, as she listened to a bald man with a tie. Lana wondered what her mom thought of her father's dancing, but she didn't even glance his way.

Ducking under adults propped in doorways, Lana made her way to the kitchen and grabbed a slice of fruitcake from the platter.

She was reaching for a third piece when Mr Perron strode from the direction of the bedrooms, his eyes fevered. He banged his half-filled glass on the benchtop, splashing the laminex.

'Want to go skidooing?'

She stared. Surely he wouldn't just leave the party?

'You must be bored. And I could do with a breather. Check with your mom.' He opened a cupboard near the back door and pulled out coats, snowpants, boots and gloves. 'Here. You're not much smaller than Yvette.' He wasn't staggering or slurring his words.

She felt a dart of fear, then a buzzing excitement.

She crept into the living room, slipping through the fog of smoke and sweat. On the couch beside the bald man, her mother lolled against the cushions. Her father twirled the kindergarten teacher, dipping her low and grinning as she squealed. No one spoke to Lana, or even looked at her. She waited a minute, then hurried back. 'Mom says it's fine.'

She pulled on the jacket and pants and stepped into boots. Mr Perron wrote a note and fixed it to the counter with a bottle: *Gone skidooing.* She wrapped a scarf around her neck, and put on gloves and a knit cap. Neither of them suggested she get her own things from the bedroom.

~

Though the snow had stopped, the night air was piercing, blowing under Lana's scarf, slicing at her neck. The snowmobile roared beneath them and she clung to Mr Perron's waist. He pointed off to the right; he was heading for the lake. She nodded, ducking behind him against the wind.

The lake was where people in Taloka went to skidoo. Sometimes they played hockey too – high schoolers who thought they were Lanny McDonald, or some other Maple Leaf hotshot. It was frozen solid now, but every winter there were accidents when people tried the ice too early. Last year the brother of a kid in her class had drowned.

They sped along the shoulder of the road, keeping clear of the mounds of snow pushed up by the ploughs, then veered off onto the trail that led to the lake. She imagined her parents finding the note and her pulse surged.

Then she remembered her dad dancing, and her mother sunk deep in the couch. They wouldn't even know she was gone.

The snowmobile bumped down towards the lake's edge. Her cheeks were tight and cold above her scarf, and she knew she'd have frostbite later – a white line of frozen flesh that would make her mother sigh. It had happened before. No big deal.

Mr Perron turned and gestured, index finger circling in the air. A lap of the lake. Lana shuddered as she gave a thumbs up.

The moonlight was bright on the snow, and the lake shone like a pearl. They lurched down the incline and onto the flat of the lake where they slowed, then stopped, the snowmobile still grumbling.

'You alright there?'

Mr Perron didn't have kids, and she wondered why. He made her feel important. Like she mattered.

'Yep!' she yelled over the idling motor. Her teeth chattered under the scarf.

'Okay then.' He pressed the throttle and they moved off smoothly, heading to the left in a gentle arc.

The moon hung above the lake, a silvery sun in the grey evening sky. It was unnaturally light, a strange day-night that reminded her of a dream. Beneath their bodies, the machine screamed across the vast whiteness and curved to hug the tree-dotted shore.

Their track unrolled behind them – a long, glistening line that followed them like a friend. Lana tipped her head back to scan the sky, dizzy with happiness, holding Mr Perron and flying through the night.

She blinked away tears as they careened to the right, completing the loop. They rose up the shore and back onto the trail, where he paused.

'How was that?' His voice was uneven.

'It was cool. Really cool.'

'Good. Now let's get you home.' They charged towards the road, rocking and bouncing over the snow.

The light faded as clouds clumped across the moon. Mr Perron hunched forward, and she had to lean to keep close. Just before the road, a streak of movement caught her eye. A snowshoe hare, fat and white, jumped across the trail. Mr Perron flinched, turning the handlebars. The hare stopped and seemed to look at Lana before bounding away.

They veered crazily off the path. The snowmobile wobbled and slipped. Mr Perron yelled something – she could feel the vibrations in his ribs – then they went over, sliding and turning. Her whole world spun and rolled and she couldn't tell which way was up. She screamed, 'Stop! Stop!' With a jolt and a crack they were still.

The skidoo sat crumpled against a tree. Mr Perron lay curled on the far side of the trunk, hands in his lap and his head bowed strangely low.

She'd been flung free too, though her leg hurt where she'd been dragged beneath the machine. The sound of her own breathing filled her ears, quick and rasping. She crawled towards Mr Perron. Partway there, a clod of snow fell from a branch down the back of her parka. She began to shake.

'Mr Perron!' Lana took his hand, bending close. His eyes were shut, and he was still. 'Hey! Wake up!' She tugged at his wrist, looking about.

The darkness was dense around her. The snowmobile's headlight still burned, facing the lake.

'M-Mister Per-ron.' She swiped at her eyes with a glove, water icing her lashes.

He didn't move.

She pushed herself to stand, her whole body quaking. Up the hill, a truck swept past, air brakes engaging with a hiss as it curved around the bend.

She stumbled towards the road. Her feet were like bricks and her left leg ached. Reaching the highway, she ran a hand along the ploughed-up mounds for guidance. Snow coated her scarf; the wool was wet across her mouth. It was taking so long to get back, and she couldn't stop crying.

A set of headlights approached through the night and she waved wildly. The vehicle came level, the passenger door opened, and her mother scrambled out.

'Lana! Oh my god! Are you okay?'

She sobbed into her mom's camel-hair coat.

'Come on, let's get you in the car.'

'But Mr Perron …'

'Where is he? What's happened?'

Lana pointed to the lake, unable to speak. Her mother's face changed.

'Okay. Hop in. We'll look after this.'

Her dad leapt out, and Lana eased herself into the station wagon, her leg throbbing, shutting the door to keep in the warmth. Outside, her parents yelled at each other back and forth. Finally, her mom jumped into the driver's seat, and her dad grabbed a torch and disappeared. Her mother drove back to the Perrons' house, hands rigid on the wheel.

~

An ambulance shrieked out to the lake, its siren raising goose-bumps down Lana's arms. Not long after, her father trudged into the dining room where the last guests toyed with limp crackers. He still wore his boots and his hair was wild. He stopped before Mrs Perron and shook his head.

She raised her hands to her mouth. 'No. No.'

'I'm so sorry, Yvette.'

Her face twisted and she turned away. 'Oh goddamn it. Goddamn that stupid man!'

Mr Kondos walked towards her but she stepped back, pointing. 'Don't touch me!'

Lana's mom sat Mrs Perron on the couch, rubbing her back as she crumpled. The others spoke in low voices.

Her father gathered some short, fat glasses and poured golden-brown drinks. Mr Kondos stared at Mrs Perron. He reminded Lana of a dog wanting food.

Although she was warm, Lana shivered in her chair. She felt sick, like that time she had the flu.

She saw Mr Perron, folded in the snow.

Her stomach rolled, and her mouth watered like it always did before she puked. She slid off her chair and hurried down the hall, past the shadowed guest room and into the bathroom, bright with flowered wallpaper.

She clutched the toilet, her knees wobbly on the tiles and the smell of Lysol in her throat. Sweat prickled across her lip. She retched and gagged, but nothing came up. Pulling a wad of toilet paper, she wiped her mouth and flushed.

As she washed her hands, she heard her teacher begin to weep, the cries rippling down the hall and rising to a howl. Lana's hands froze on the plush peach handtowel. She breathed slowly through her nose.

'Here you are. Are you alright?' Her father stroked the side of her cheek, just a wisp of touch. She reached out to him, pulling closer, until her head pressed hard against his chest.

'It's okay, honey. You're okay.'

She nodded.

In her reflection she saw the pale lines of frostbite, etched just below her eyes.

BOXING DAY

NADINE PLACED A HAND ON Herc's chest. Above the bed, the fan stirred tropical air. 'We should have sex,' she said, 'since we didn't for Christmas.'

Herc raised his eyebrows. 'Wow, what an offer.' He began to lift her fingers one by one, flexing them back a little too far, so that she pulled her hand away.

'Herc, don't.'

They lay in the clear morning light, a fine sweat beading their bodies. They'd turned off the air conditioner the first day here, to soak up the balmy weather.

Herc closed his eyes and his breathing deepened. Below their room, someone swept the path, a rhythmic *swish, swish.*

Nadine touched his shoulder. 'I'm going to breakfast. Maybe a swim after that. You coming?' She slid off the bed and dressed quickly in swimsuit, dress and sandals.

Herc yawned, starfished on the sheets. 'Might sleep a bit.'

Nadine picked up her towel and beach bag. She paused. 'See you soon?'

'Sure.' Herc's voice faded into the pillow.

~

The Patong Beach Glorious Hotel was four-star and fancy, but Thailand was cheap and Nadine had found a bargain. The hotel was opposite the water, with private balconies and ocean views.

Nadine sat sipping her coffee in the open-air dining. All around her, couples talked and played with each other's hands. At the end of the verandah one pair leant to kiss across the table. Most were younger – on honeymoon, she supposed. Not like her and Herc, together eight years and still in some sort of limbo.

'More coffee, madam?' The waiter held up the pot.

'Thank you.' She lifted the cup to her lips, gazing out to the blue of Patong Bay. This place was idyllic. She should be happy. But soon the year would be over, another one slipped through her fingers.

She pulled her bag onto her shoulder as she stood.

'Have a nice day, madam.' The waiter was the same young man she'd seen every day so far – same starched white jacket, the same polite face. She wondered what he thought of her, beneath his good manners. Did he find her ridiculous, with her crumpled dress and pale-as-dough limbs? Was he disgusted by her eating, swimming and dozing while he worked?

'Thank you –' she paused to read his name badge '– Kiet.' Why hadn't she used his name before now? She hurried out before she could see his expression, crossing the road and following the path through the trees. On the beach, warm sand spilled into her sandals.

The sign near the lifeguard chair was the same as the day before: *Fine, good swimming. Be careful to wear sunscreen.* The tall chair was unoccupied. She'd never seen a lifeguard, didn't know why the chair was there. Perhaps it featured on the website – a comfort for nervous swimmers – she couldn't remember. She'd booked this trip in a last-minute rush, hoping a holiday would help.

Christmas was her least favourite time of year, family all asking when she and Herc would marry, when they'd have children. At the start, she'd been excited by the questions, but now they made her uneasy. Was this what couples did? Stayed together long enough that marriage was next? Had kids because that seemed to follow?

The beach was scattered with people, most in pairs. She squinted behind her sunglasses, wishing she'd worn a hat. Along the rows of umbrella-topped beach chairs, one was still free. She made a beeline for it, head down. But as she reached the chair, a leopard-print towel landed on the seat.

A thin woman in a black bikini smiled widely. 'Gotta be quick around here.' She slipped into the chair and eased back, closing her eyes.

Nadine sighed and moved down the shore, spreading her towel in the shade of a clump of trees. She kicked off her sandals and sat propped on her hands, legs extended. There were plenty of people, but hardly anyone was moving. Just a few children laughed and dug with spades.

The heat was stifling, even beneath the trees. Waves of warmth swelled from the sand. Back in Hobart, she'd longed for hot weather, for perspiration and relaxed, loose muscles, but now she suddenly wished herself home. The thought of cool air on her skin brought tears to her eyes.

This was crazy. She was supposed to be happy – no work for an entire week, and time with Herc. They were supposed to be unwinding. Reconnecting.

A seagull landed just in front of her, pecking at something half-buried in the sand. Between bites, it stood with one foot lifted. The foot was deformed, just a stump with one claw.

'What happened?' Nadine asked. 'Are you alright, bird?' The gull cocked its head, and returned to tearing at the food.

She shaded her eyes, looking past the bird to the ocean. The water appeared unusually far away, the beach wider than she'd seen it. The three longboats anchored in a row sat high and dry, their ropes limp. All along the beach, driftwood and clumps of seaweed dotted the shoreline, extending to the sea.

Herc emerged from the tree-lined path, his hair still spiky at the crown. He marched towards her, ignoring a small boy who called to him, holding up some treasure – a stone, or a shell.

'What's the deal with the tide?' Herc asked, glancing at the vast stretch of sand.

Nadine shrugged. 'I don't know. It's a long way out.' Her scalp itched with irritation. She made room on her towel and they sat shoulder to shoulder. The silence between them was as sticky as the air. Maybe she should try harder. Maybe they could revive this somehow.

'I'm sorry about before, what I said.' Nadine brushed sand from her shin. 'I'm no good at being sexy.'

Herc leant into her. 'It's fine. I'm used to you.'

Anger flared in her cheeks and she considered saying he was no sex god himself, the way he cut his toenails on the couch and used the bathroom with the door open. She shifted so their bodies didn't touch.

A breeze blew in from the water. Beside them the injured seagull hopped around, searching for tidbits. The feathers at its throat were stained yellow. Now and then it gave a plaintive squawk. Nadine felt tears well again, and she wiped them as they slipped below her glasses.

Herc used the resigned tone he often took if she cried. 'What's up, Deens?'

His big handsome face blurred. She had loved him, in the beginning. 'Can't you tell things aren't right?'

Herc's jaw tightened. He stared out to sea.

The seagull yanked a crust from the sand and flapped away.

'You're comparing us, aren't you – to those honeymoon couples.' Herc shook his head. 'We've been together seven years, what do you expect?'

'Eight years.'

'What?'

'We've been together eight years.' Nadine drew her knees up, wrapping her arms around her legs.

Raised voices drifted down the beach, strident and harsh. She thought it must be the day for arguments.

'Herc.' Her voice cracked and she tried again. 'I want to feel romantic after twenty years. Thirty years. Not all the time, but sometimes.'

Herc was focused on the horizon. He rose to his feet.

'Herc?'

The clamour from the hotel was louder, and Nadine turned to see several people approaching. One was Kiet. His jacket flapped open at the neck as he waved his arms in the air.

'Run!' he yelled. 'Run to hotel!' He seemed flustered, but Nadine could see no reason for his distress. Other beachgoers were standing up, appearing as confused as she was.

Herc pointed to the ocean, his voice full of wonder. 'Look.'

Nadine stood and at first saw nothing but the shining waters of

Patong Bay. Then she noticed a long line of white – an incredible unbroken crest.

'Run, run!' Kiet was yelling at guests in sun loungers. 'To hotel!'

Herc glanced at Nadine, and she saw her fear reflected in his eyes. She grabbed her bag and they rushed up the beach.

'Where will we go? The hotel roof?' Nadine panted, stumbling in the sand.

'Anywhere high.' Herc jogged easily beside her.

To one side, an old woman struggled up from her beach chair, grappling with a cane. Her hair hung in grey strands as she pushed herself straight. 'Mais …?' she asked the space around her. 'Pourquoi?'

Nadine looked for Kiet, hoping he would help the woman, but she spotted him ahead with a mother and children, carrying a toddler in his arms.

Panic swamped her mind. She could pretend she hadn't seen.

Nadine hurried to the old lady, and reached for her elbow.

'Lean on us, we'll take you.' She glanced around for Herc. He wasn't there.

Through the surging crowd, she glimpsed him at the path, head swivelled her way, mouth wide. She thought he shouted, 'Leave her!' but there was so much noise, she couldn't be sure. He ran on.

There was a strange stillness in her chest. She took a sharp, painful breath. Wrapping an arm around the woman, Nadine steered her towards the track.

Sweat dripped into Nadine's eyes. The old lady moved quickly, despite her limp. She huffed as they walked. 'Merci, merci.'

Nadine nodded. 'That's right, fast, fast.' They turned onto the path, and people pushed past them, jostling and screaming.

There was a sound now, like the rumble of a plane. Nadine tilted her face to the empty sky and her skin grew cold.

She didn't look back, just kept tugging the old lady. She pulled her along and told her, 'Good, that's good,' as the roaring filled her ears.

AND YOU MAY ASK YOURSELF

SANJAY STANDS BY THE WALL in the dining room, keeping clear of people hovering near platters. The house is warm and stuffy, mourners filling the lounge room and flowing through to the kitchen, where conversations near the coffee urn are strangely cheery. He recognises no one except Warren's mother, who sits gripping a mug, her expression dazed. It's been years since Sanjay visited Toowoomba.

The place has changed, he saw that driving into town – new businesses, houses and renovations. There's a Coles now on James Street. People queuing for coffee at a fancy café where once there was just a fibro shack. And when he rolled past the old brick house, the jacaranda he'd once climbed stretched its thick grey arms above a garage extension. He peered up at the living-room window, neck tingling with the crazy notion that his mother would appear. A young man walked out the front door, waving back to a woman and baby, and Sanjay drove on.

But Warren's childhood home seems untouched by time. It still has the faint smell of dried apple. Crystal birds and ceramic ladies sit on the shelves. Above the fireplace, the glass-domed clock chimes the quarter hour. Sanjay remembers how he and Warren would spread their books across the table, do homework, play music and talk a bunch of crap – things they couldn't do at Sanjay's place because his father worked nights at the abattoir. Mrs Haig would slip a plate of buttered Saos between the boys, asking about their day, and Sanjay would eat doggedly, the crackers pulpy in his throat.

Sanjay peers at the photos on the sideboard. Warren as a plump-cheeked baby. Warren as a schoolboy, in his checked, collared shirt – the shirt he'd untuck as he and Sanjay dawdled home from school, tossing a footy back and forth, believing they had all the time in the world. Warren in a graduation gown. Warren and Linda on their wedding day, outside St Luke's, where Sanjay spent the past half hour, standing and sitting and murmuring hymns. In each image, Warren grins broadly, his smile reaching beyond the frame. Sanjay swallows and turns away.

A teenage boy has squeezed in alongside him and is leaning on the wall like someone waiting for a bus. The kid looks crushed, and Sanjay wonders if he's Warren's nephew, or a student Warren once taught. He knows the boy isn't Warren's, but only through his absence from photos on display. How has Sanjay not seen Warren for fifteen years? These days he has dinner with his wife's friends and goes to drinks with colleagues. He follows other people's plans.

The teenager sighs deeply. He reminds Sanjay of his youngest son, a few years back. He catches the boy's gaze. 'I'm sorry for your loss.'

The boy looks startled, mumbling something inaudible.

He clears his throat. 'I'm Sanjay. I went to school with

Warren.' Beyond the back window, the lawn is the same trim square of grass where he and Warren tinkered with their bikes, patching up tyres and tightening brakes. They used to ride those bikes flat out – mostly for fun, sometimes to escape the Miller boys who'd yell at Sanjay to go back where he came from.

'Uh, hi. I'm Titan.' Titan pushes off the wall, offers a hand. 'I, uh, don't actually know Warren.' He rubs an ear. 'I just drove my dad here.'

'Oh, right.' Sanjay decides the boy's hangdog appearance springs from gaping boredom.

Titan folds his arms, unfolds them. 'Dad's lost his licence.' He looks around, colouring. 'Don't, like, tell anyone.'

Sanjay nods. 'No problem.'

A silence falls. Sanjay considers, then abandons, observations on the weather. Before he can stumble out a school-related question, the boy pulls a mobile from his pocket, taps the screen. 'So, uh, do you follow cricket?'

Sanjay pauses. People are surprised and often disappointed by his lack of interest in cricket. They want him to be different in other ways too. Warren was the first person, besides family, to make him feel okay just as he was.

Titan blurts, 'We're losing against New Zealand! Can you believe it?' He holds up the phone, displaying the score. 'It's completely fucked.'

An older woman looks sharply their way, and Sanjay smiles until she moves on, lamington in hand.

'I'm sorry to hear that,' Sanjay says, and he really is. The kid is at that age of awkwardness and raging passions, vulnerable to every disappointment.

'Yeah, it sucks.' Titan lunges forward, grabbing a handful of mini sausage rolls.

~

As he swallows the last mouthful and wipes his hands on his chinos, Titan's relieved to see his dad hugging the dead guy's mum, saying goodbye. His dad promised him the car if he did taxi duty here and back to Brisbane, and Titan has a full afternoon planned. He's going to hit the coast with Marley, get a last surf in before school starts next week.

'Alright, mate. Let's head.' His father stands before him, doesn't acknowledge Sanjay. His breath is heavy with beer. Titan gets that familiar ping of nerves, though he knows things will be alright. He's taller and stronger than his dad now.

He nods at Sanjay. 'See you later.'

Sanjay smiles. 'Nice to meet you, Titan.'

Titan and his dad make their way down the front steps and out to the car. His father yanks open the passenger door. 'So who's the Indian?'

Titan shrugs and gets in, fumbling with the keys. 'Just a guy. Said he went to school with Warren.'

His father slams the door. 'Ha. Bet he hardly knew him.' His cheeks are pink. 'We knew Warren, at the dojo. Especially us black belts.' He drags the seatbelt across and clicks it in place. 'Come on, let's go!'

Titan is surprised to see his father's eyes are wet.

He drives the Warrego Highway smooth and easy. His dad pulls on sunglasses and falls asleep. He looks peaceful, even friendly. Maybe he would have been that type of man, if Titan's mum was still alive.

Titan was eight, no baby, when she died, but he can't remember much from the years before. Sometimes fragments return – his mum pushing him on a swing, his dad lighting candles on a cake. Nothing more than fleeting moments. Since then, it's been him and his dad and his dad's drinking. Titan tries to stay away. He hangs out with Marley and his other mates. Works at Macca's. When he can, he surfs.

Titan holds the wheel with one hand, his elbow out the window. He pictures perfect waves rolling in, the rise and crest and barrel.

Almost two hours later, they're back in Brisbane. His dad sleeps through the stop-start traffic, waking only when they pull up outside the repair shop. He climbs out with his work bag, unsteady at first. Titan watches, shame creeping up his neck.

Once his dad has disappeared inside, Titan rounds the corner fast. His heart pumps with new energy. One stop, then Snapper Rocks.

He's not far from Marley's when he sees the pharmacy sign and slows. Last surf he got fried – red and blistered on his face and arms. He turns and parks.

Inside, the store is cool and quiet. Titan wanders past shampoo and hair dye, bandaids and ear plugs. Finally, he finds the sunscreen. Lotion, spray, roll-on? Sensitive?

'Hi there, can I help?' The woman's badge says *Mandy*. Her face is wide and freckled, with fine lines across her forehead. Something flickers in his chest. His mum had freckles too. The same listening eyes.

He has a sudden urge to blurt it all out, to tell the woman all the bullshit he's been through. The shouting, the beltings. The silent days.

The woman waits. She looks calm and kind.

'Nah, I'm good.' He picks up the cheapest bottle. Soon he'll be in the water, practising his frontside carves.

'Okay.' She smiles, and moves off to help an old man.

~

Mandy watches the boy from the corner of her eye as he tosses the sunscreen hand to hand, strolling to the till. He's younger than her sons, but he's the same build – lanky and lean – with a brittle bravado that pricks at her heart. The boy pays and walks out to a battered old car.

When he's gone, Mandy checks the time. It's nearly two o'clock, the end of her shift.

Driving home, she lets the breeze warm her skin. The poincianas are in bloom up and down the street, the flowers flame-red against bright green leaves. She parks outside their house, and pats the dogs as they greet her at the gate.

Opening the door, she calls out, 'Hi-ya, anyone home?' The words rebound in the empty house. It's only been six days, and sometimes she forgets. In the kitchen, everything is as she left it – dishwasher closed, sink clean, cupboards shut. So much tidiness it hurts her eyes.

She puts her bag down and pulls out her phone. She hasn't heard from Patrick since they helped him move. She'll just text him – something light, maybe *How's the new digs?* But no, that's not right, he'll think she's lame. She heard him say that to his brothers at Christmas, that something old-fashioned was *lame*. But that's her, really, isn't it? She's fifty-four and she's never going to be in fashion, not anymore. The best she can hope for is not to embarrass her sons too much.

She deletes the draft message and tries again. *How are things?* In her mind's eye she sees the house her youngest has moved into with his friends, an old place with faded paint and crooked front steps. She hopes he's eating decent food, not pizza and soft drink every night. She hopes he isn't sick, or unhappy. How will she know now?

Quickly she types, *Making a roast on Sunday, come if you can,* and sends the text. She picks up her novel and stretches out on the couch, phone beside her. There's no reply, and she imagines Patrick sighing, devising an excuse.

She tries to read, then lets the book fall onto her lap. Soon she'll walk the dogs, put out the bins and start dinner. Eventually her husband will come home. She'll ask about his day, serve up two meals, and the vacant chairs will watch them as they eat.

~

Sanjay stares out the window of the high-rise, his thoughts anywhere but on the spreadsheet. The afternoon is turning slowly to evening, the clouds to the west tipped with orange. He's not getting work done. Every time he looks at the figures, his office dissolves, and he's riding down Mount Rascal Road with Warren, grinning as they pick up speed, Sanjay so happy he lets out a long, loud whoop and Warren laughing so much that he swerves and almost stacks it.

Sanjay closes his laptop. He picks up his bag, and heads for the lift. In the car, he searches his playlist until he finds the Talking Heads song, spiralling up through the concrete car park with 'Once in a Lifetime' blasting in his ears. He tries to sing along, but his throat closes on the music, just his tongue and lips forming words as he asks himself how he got here. As he asks himself what he's done.

Warren used to shout the song, like a schoolkid preacher guiding the world.

What was he thinking, at the end? What made him decide he'd had enough?

Traffic is heavy, and Sanjay crawls along, music swilling through the car. He gives up trying to sing. It's hard to see the road.

When the song clicks over Sanjay wipes his face. The freeway is clearing now and as the car glides over bitumen he listens to more music on his playlist – songs his sons suggested, Coldplay, classics from Queen.

He parks in the carport and checks in the mirror. His eyes look normal, just the usual end-of-the-day redness. He strides to the front door and lets himself in, the smell of chicken casserole rising to greet him.

He's known his wife since his university days. They've been together so long, she's as familiar as his own skin. He loves her with a comfortable affection.

'Hi, hon,' he calls. Usually he takes his bag through to the bedroom, but today he drops it near the door and finds Mandy in the kitchen, just closing the oven.

Sanjay pulls her in tight and Mandy returns the hug with oven-mitted hands. 'Was it awful?' she says.

Sanjay rests his cheek on her smooth, warm hair. 'I just …' He swallows. 'I thought I'd see him again.'

'I know.' Mandy's voice vibrates in his sternum.

He's glad she doesn't say, 'It's not your fault' or 'How could you have predicted this?' because he's thought it through. All these years without contact, and no good excuse.

He releases her, scans the day's mail. 'How are you?'

Sanjay knows she's having a rough time, with Patrick gone, but they'll still see their son. He's proud that all three boys are making their way in the world.

'I'm alright,' Mandy says, but her mouth does a strange twist as she turns to peer into the oven. 'I just miss him, you know?'

Her phone beeps on the benchtop and Sanjay picks it up, hands it over.

Mandy clicks on the message and her face lights up. 'It's Patrick. I asked him for Sunday dinner. He says, *See you then.*'

Sanjay nods. 'He's a good kid.'

He thinks of Warren as a boy, a teen, an adult, his life reduced to photos on a sideboard. Sanjay takes his bag through to the bedroom, changes into shorts and T-shirt. He sits on the bed, head bowed.

He knows he is lucky. His wife, his boys, a decent job. But he remembers the glory of his youth. Big friendships and adventures. Heady, passionate love. The potential to be remarkable. He longs for all that brightness.

His life feels so much smaller now.

Mandy calls from the kitchen, 'Sanjay! Dinner!' and he lifts his gaze to his reflection in the mirrored wardrobe doors. He runs a hand across his bald spot and calls to his wife, 'Okay!' but he stays a moment longer.

ONE SUNDAY AFTERNOON

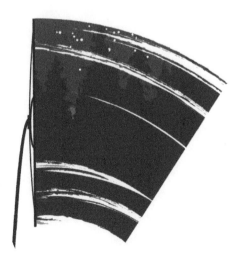

Zach stands straight, feet apart, hands in pockets. His toes tap inside his runners. His girlfriend, Francine, flicks the brake on the cot wheel – up, down, up, down. She consults the price tag.

There are people everywhere – talking, pointing, yawning, trailing fingers over furniture. Children whine and cry and run from their parents. The ceiling is too low for such a large space and the lighting is too bright.

Zach's urge to leave is getting stronger by the minute, but it's nothing to do with what happened in 2009. Every time he feels like getting out of a place – a café, a shop, the gym – Francine gives him a knowing look, and it drives him crazy. It's been over three years. He's not like the guys who see the army shrinks. He sleeps well at night, doesn't jump at loud noises. And he doesn't panic inside buildings. Sometimes he wants to get going, same as always, because he's bored. Or hungry, like now. It's been two hours since lunch.

He steps closer, puts a hand on the small of Francine's back. 'Want to get a snack?'

Francine spins around. 'What? No.' Her belly is still neat and round, like a helmet strapped to her tiny frame. 'We've only just started.' She flips a lever and the side of the cot clatters down.

~

That Sunday he banged the alarm clock quiet in his bunker room. It was just another mission out of Tarin Kowt.

He'd been in Camp Holland five months. The dry heat and dust were relentless, but he'd adjusted, he was doing his job. He trusted the guys in his team.

They'd left at dawn in the Bushmaster, headed to the drop-off point, then spent the day on dismounted patrol in the Mirabad Valley.

It was getting late, the sun crouching low as they trudged through the cornfield. They were almost at their pick-up point.

Zach was out front with the junior sapper, Siggy, searching for IEDs. They were in good spirits. The day had gone well. They'd spoken with tribal elders in Musazi, given them school supplies and first-aid kits.

The corn around them was waist high, waving in the breeze. They were all in that state of relaxed attentiveness, alert to any movement nearby. Watching the hills too, for insurgent spotters or snipers.

Zach and Siggy checked the ground for freshly turned soil.

~

'Check this out, Zach. It converts into a bed.'

Zach nods. He wants Francine to be happy. She's stuck with him through everything, waited almost a year when he was deployed. They're having a baby because she thought it was time, said they were both twenty-six, why not, and he agreed. But sometimes when he thinks about the unborn kid, a stab of pain twists in his temple.

Francine slides a hand along the glossy white paintwork. 'Do you like it?'

'Sure. Yeah.' He tries to sound enthused. Maybe they can buy it and leave, get sundaes on the way home.

Francine retracts her arm. 'Let's just go.' He realises he hasn't shown real interest, hasn't asked about features or cost.

She heads off, practically sprinting.

He follows, avoiding the gaze of a couple stretched out on a mattress. 'Babe. Wait.' It's hard to keep pace. Francine's legs are much shorter and Zach should catch up in seconds but she's agile and quick, ducking past beds and dressing tables. In the aisle, large, black arrows on the floor point the way deeper into the beast.

He finally draws level. Her face is like a fortress.

The room narrows and they turn into another vast cavern filled with kitchens in tan and white. People swarm in and out of the displays, snooping in cupboards and yanking out drawers. Zach surveys the surrounds.

~

Some combat engineers couldn't handle it, being out front, scanning the ground for explosives. They got the jitters, lost their nerve. He never suffered from that. He was scared, for sure, but it gave him a high too, that fear, every time the unit went on patrol.

Clearing the way for the boys in the cornfield that day, he was more alive than ever. Could feel every pump of his heart. The scuff of his boots, the swish of his fatigues, the huff of breath - they resounded in his head as he swung the mine detector in a slow arc, side to side.

Corn grew all the way to a line of scrubby sage bush to their left. On their right, the crop stretched towards a low wall and a few stunted almond trees bordering the next field. The mountains flanked the valley, rising beige and bald beyond the green belt.

Zach's feet sank into sandy soil as he passed between rows and the backs of his hands brushed the plants. The sweet smell of young leaves rose up all around. A faint breeze cooled his neck. The heat of the day was fading.

~

The store is too hot, so many people. Zach walks beside Francine, dodging giant trolleys. She's not talking. When she's like this, he feels more and more helpless, unable to work out what she needs.

Somehow they're in another chamber of this never-ending store, a room full of glassware and tablecloths. But at the far end, exit signs appear. Francine storms past the registers and out the door, almost colliding with a man and his toddler son.

At the car, Zach smiles at Francine but she hops into the passenger seat and shuts the door.

'Hungry?' he asks, but she doesn't reply. He reverses in one fluid motion, drives out of the parking lot and heads for home. Winding down the windows, he lets cool air flood between them.

~

Zach was teasing Siggy, asking did he want a jumper – the guy felt cold at twenty-two degrees – when the first shot rang out. There was nowhere to hide, they were fifty metres from the wall with only cornstalks for cover. Zach dropped to the ground, heard the thumps of others doing the same.

There was a crack in the mud wall, he could see the barrel of a rifle through his binoculars. They'd all be mown down if they didn't move.

Zach motioned his intentions to Siggy. He began to leopard crawl towards the shooter.

More gunfire erupted and his team answered fire, but the Taliban fighter was protected by the wall. Every time Zach moved, he thought of IEDs concealed beneath the dirt, pictured his body exploding in the air – a mess of red.

A bullet hissed by his shoulders.

'Fuck! My leg!' Siggy's face was stretched with panic. A small circle of blood bloomed on his pants, but the stain wasn't spreading.

'Stay there. Use your pressure dressing.' Zach

held Siggy's gaze. The kid was only twenty, same
as Zach's little brother. 'You'll be okay. Just keep
your head down.'

Siggy nodded, and Zach hustled forward. He had
to get within thirty metres. He could do it, he was
almost there.

~

'I don't even know where you are these days.' Francine stares out
the passenger window.

Zach steers with one hand, cruising along the freeway. A
light rain has started, drops spattering the windscreen. The sky is
growing dark.

'Babe …' He knows what she means, at least partly. 'I'm right
here, with you.'

Francine speaks in a way he hasn't heard before – mild yet
determined. 'I know you think that. And your body's here. But a
lot of the time *you're* not.' She fiddles with the seatbelt. 'Sometimes
I feel like …' Francine lapses into silence.

Zach waits. 'You feel like?'

'No, nothing.'

He's irritated now. He flicks the indicator, changes lanes to
pass a cattle truck. They overtake the semitrailer, the animals
crushed in together, showing the whites of their eyes.

Francine's hand moves to her face and Zach looks across. A
tear slides down her cheek.

~

Sweat ran down his forehead and into his eyes. His
arms and legs burned. He was close enough now.

Zach reached along his chest rig, pulled the grenade from its pouch. Grasping it firmly, he removed the pin, then kneeled up and threw. A bullet pinged off his helmet. He flung himself flat.

The explosion roared up and echoed in his ears. Stones and dust and fragments of the packed-earth wall rained down, knocking at his helmet, stinging his hands, pelting his back and legs. There was silence for several seconds, all the men waiting. When Zach raised his head, he saw the cloud of debris on the far side of the wall and the relief left him trembling.

He waited another ten seconds. There were no further shots.

Zach approached the wall. The team fell in behind him, all except Siggy and the medic.

At the wall, Zach kept low and to the side of the damaged section. As he moved along, he checked for telltale signs of IEDs. The men followed, faces powdered with dirt.

Zach reached the gap where the grenade had done its work. All was quiet. Rifle held ready, he peered through to the adjacent field.

Just beyond the ruined wall, a man lay on his back, his remaining arm flung out. His tunic was dark with blood. Rifle pieces lay scattered nearby. The arsehole was dead.

Zach reported in. 'He's down. Fighting-age male down.'

Then a flutter caught Zach's eye, and he swivelled

to the right, levelling his rifle at the movement.

The boy was crumpled in a ball, half covered in dry earth. He looked seven or maybe eight years old. His shirt hem lifted and fell in the breeze.

~

The windscreen wipers thrash back and forth, not quite keeping the field of vision clear. Zach takes their exit, steers smoothly through blurry streets.

They pull into the carport. Water runs down the windscreen in tiny channels.

Rain drums above them, a torrential Brisbane downpour.

'Zach. The man you were before …' Francine sniffs, and digs around in her bag, pulling a tissue from a packet. 'I don't think he came back.'

Zach's hands don't move from his legs. He breathes evenly in, carefully out.

~

'Holy fuck.' He whispered it as he clambered across the broken foundations. 'Fuck, fuck.'

'Watch your feet!' The bark of the corporal through his headset brought Zach to his senses. He slowed down, scrutinised the ground as he advanced.

'There's a kid!' he relayed back.

Zach knelt close. No movement, no breathing.

Holding the shoulder, Zach turned the boy. The child's face gazed to the sky, eyes open, unblinking.

Zach clutched the torn shirt. He could hear his corporal talking in his earpiece. The boy had eyebrows so feathery and fine — dark wings above his deep brown eyes.

~

'I'm not blaming you, Zach.' Francine has turned, trying to catch his eye. 'What you must have been through. The things you can't tell me.' She takes his hand, strokes it with her thumb. A gutter on the house is overflowing now, splashing onto the brick terrace.

Zach pulls the keys from the ignition. It's been three years, four months. He'd told Francine about that day, told her it didn't end well. He wasn't allowed to say more.

In his mind he sees the small, dusty face.

He won't tell her everything, just the part that matters.

Zach clears his throat. 'There was this boy.'

PLUME

LORI SAT WITH HER BACK against the bed, the phone pulled under the door. She was talking to Travis Dunn, but he was quiet, in fact he hadn't spoken for a while. Now and then he sighed, a rush of need down the line.

The house was stuffy though it was only May, and Lori remembered the weatherman last week, predicting the coming summer as the hottest in years. Weird things were happening lately – earthquakes near the coast and a mountain puffing steam to the west. Her parents kept discussing the record rain forecast for Washington state, with big falls expected even out here on the plains. The land seemed uneasy and off balance. She moved the receiver to the other ear.

'Travis? I gotta go. Mom needs me.' Her parents and sister weren't home from church yet, but he wouldn't know. She inched up the volume on her radio cassette, tapping her foot to Blondie's 'Call Me'.

'Okay.' His tone was mournful, same as every time she ended their conversations.

'Bye, Travis.'

He didn't answer and Lori got up, opening her door. She slid the cord free and carried the phone into her parents' gloomy bedroom. Just before she hung up, Travis murmured, 'Wait.'

She stopped, gripping the receiver.

'What about next Friday?'

'Next Friday?' She couldn't stand another night with Travis curled around her on his basement couch, holding her hand with big, sweaty fingers, breathing on her neck.

'Are we going to ...'

'No. I don't think so.' Lori twisted the spiral cord around her thumb, over and over until the tip turned a deep purple-red.

His silence was heavy, sticky as molasses. She placed the receiver in its cradle with a click.

~

Lori poked her head into the hall. Her sister, Angela, sat at the kitchen table in her navy dress, pencils spread around, drawing on her science poster. Lori's dad bumped around in the next room, opening and closing drawers, getting changed like he always did the second he got home. Her mother would be lying on the sofa, hair in neat curls and a washcloth across her eyes. Church always seemed to bring on her sick headaches. Lori had asked why she kept going, and her mother just said, 'It's the right thing, that's why.'

Lori slipped back into her room, wrote a note and left it on the dresser, pinned down by the snow globe Angela had given her last Christmas. She snuck out the back door, dragging her bike from the carport.

None of her so-called friends liked to ride bikes anymore. They talked hairstyles and nail polish and 'doing it' with boys.

They had sleepovers and bitched about girls who weren't there. At school they laughed in a new way, high and sharp, turning their flicked hair to see who was watching.

Her parents had changed too. They used to let her ride around Harrington, now they said they didn't want her roaming all over town. Fifteen was too old, they said. People would talk. But people always talked, no matter what you did.

Lori pedalled to the road, heading south. The day was warm and sunny. After their house and the cemetery opposite, there was nothing for miles but the yellow-green wheat and the big bold sky. As Lori picked up speed, her mind flew free.

It was funny her parents thought she was wandering the town, because whenever she could, she left it behind. Even if she rode through the main street, she was on her way somewhere beyond. Sometimes she headed west, cutting past the repair shop and the low brick church her family was so nuts about, turning left onto the highway – really just a two-lane road in the middle of nowhere.

But travelling south was the best. Lori rolled along, easy as a dream. A car appeared, passed her going north, and then she was alone again. High above her, a hawk soared in slow circles, hardly moving its wings.

Lately on these rides she found herself thinking of the new girl. Joelle had started at Harrington High a month ago, but she kept to herself, taking lunchbreaks in the library. After school, she hurried to the bus, her dark braids swinging on her backpack. Yet when the teacher asked the new girl a question, she answered clearly, much louder than Lori expected.

Joelle wasn't like anyone Lori had ever met. She spoke with a faint accent. Her hair was longer than the other girls'. She wore a silver charm bracelet to school every day. And no one knew where she lived, though a few kids who caught the bus said she got off at Scott Road.

Whenever Lori found herself near Joelle – at the bathroom sinks, or in line for class – a lemony scent seemed to float in the air. Once, looking at the hollow between Joelle's neck and shoulder, Lori had felt a powerful urge to place her mouth on that skin, to feel its smooth warmth beneath her lips, to inhale the clean citrus smell. She'd stepped back, breathless.

A soft rumble distracted Lori now, growing louder. It was a red pick-up truck, coming from Harrington, going way above the speed limit. She pulled to the side, riding on rubble, but the pick-up passed her so close the engine roared in her brain, and the gust of wind made her wobble.

'Fucker!' she said, braking to a stop.

After a moment she rode on, watching the truck crest the next hill and disappear. Her heartbeat steadied and she began to relax. But as she reached the top of the rise, she saw the truck turning, kicking up dust.

The pick-up revved and her arms tensed. She clutched the handlebars and glanced back towards Harrington. Fields spanned in every direction, unbroken by tree or fence or house. The truck sped towards her. She put her feet down and told herself it was okay, she'd be okay. *The Lord is my shepherd* murmured in her brain and she desperately hoped it was true. The taste of dirt was dry on her tongue.

The pick-up was close now, slowing, dropping into second. She strained her eyes – the driver was a kid, a redhead who looked like Jude, a senior from school. And slumped in the passenger seat, could it really be? It was, she was sure. Travis stared out with his familiar sulky face.

As the truck drew almost level, it swerved towards her, and she yelped and dived off her bike, crashing to the verge of the road. The boys swung away, Jude's laughter bouncing back, with the words 'Frigid bitch!'

Lori pulled herself up on shaking legs. Her shoulder throbbed. She brushed gravel from her hands and knees, and a trickle of blood wound down one shin.

Her bike lay sprawled on the road. The truck was a blot in the distance, heading for town.

Lori was fine, nothing hurt, not really. She stood tall and crossed her arms. If they looked back, that wiener Travis and his dumbass friend, they'd see she wasn't scared. But something thrashed inside her, and she thought of the bird she'd seen while out riding last fall, one wing ground into the asphalt, still lifting its head and flapping its undamaged wing. She watched the truck until it was gone, until the flailing in her chest had eased too.

As she leant to grab her bike, she noticed a change in the light. It was fading, as if the day was ending, although it wasn't yet noon. In the southwest, a bank of clouds had gathered.

Even as Lori swung a leg across her bike, the clouds advanced – a curtain the colour of a dark, fresh bruise. She began the ride home, calf muscles straining as she rode to beat the storm. A few vehicles passed, heading the same way, but the red pick-up did not return. At last she dropped her bike in the carport and ran panting up the back steps, armpits hot and damp. She flung the door open, and it banged against the wall.

'Shut that!' her father barked. Her parents and sister were in the living room, hunched in front of the TV. The newsreader blared into the room.

The eruption occurred just after eight this morning, sending a vast mushroom cloud into the sky, and an avalanche of debris down the mountain.

'What's going on?' Lori asked, her heart still drumming in her throat.

Her father stalked to the television and cranked up the volume.

Since the explosion, the giant cloud has blown north-east, travelling swiftly with the wind. There are reports from Ellensberg of skies as black as midnight.

'What is it? What's happened?' Lori said, perched on the edge of her sister's armchair. Sweat slipped down her neck and the trembling in her bones wouldn't stop.

'Quiet!' her father snapped.

Angela knelt close to Lori, cupped her hands and whispered moistly, 'It's a volcano! Mount Helens. No, Mount *Saint* Helens.' Her face was pink with delight.

Outside, there was a dreary twilight. Angela jumped up and ran to the window. 'It's snowing!' She splayed her hands on the glass. 'Mom, come see.'

'Shhh, yes, okay.' Their mother got up, moving like a tired bear.

Lori stood beside them. Everything was layered grey – the front lawn, the mailbox, the rosebushes either side. Feathery fragments danced from the sky.

It's not yet known if the gas and ashes are harmful to the lungs. Residents of affected areas are warned to stay indoors, keep windows closed and place wet towels beneath all doors.

A sharp smoky stink had crept into the house. Lori pressed her fingertips into the windowsill, taking shallow breaths. Fear rippled down her spine. Would they die from the fumes?

Would their house be slowly buried? She wondered if Joelle was frightened too.

Her mother hustled from the room. 'Come on, girls. Let's get some towels.' They pulled a stack from the hall cupboard and wet them in the bath. Their mother plugged the front door, and Lori wedged towels beneath the back door, smoothing them over and over.

Gradually all light vanished and Lori's mother switched on the lamp. No one said much, and even Angela grew quiet. The TV broadcast finished and *M*A*S*H* began. Lori's father flicked the television off, and turned on the radio. They sat together, listening to updates on KLXY.

By mid-afternoon, the radio told listeners that earlier concerns were unfounded. The gas wasn't noxious. The ash wouldn't bury houses.

'Well that's a relief.' Lori's mother smiled for the first time that day.

Lori's father frowned, the line between his eyes cutting deep. 'Shhh.'

The announcer continued, *If going out, a mask or face covering should be worn, to prevent lung irritation.*

Was Joelle listening too, in her house?

They had something to discuss now. At their lockers, Lori could ask, 'Did you think it was a storm? I thought it was a storm!' and Joelle might say, 'Me too,' and they'd chuckle at how wrong they'd been. After that, Lori would change seats in class, to sit beside Joelle. When school was let out, she'd offer to double Joelle on her bike. Joelle could sit in front on the banana seat, her feet in the basket, and Lori would take her home if it was two miles, five miles, ten miles from town.

Lori sat back against the couch. Her mother had turned on more lights, and all Lori could see were their reflections in the windows. 'So when can we go out? What about school?'

Her father shrugged. 'I'm sure you can manage a few days without that boy.'

Lori blinked at the sudden pinching in her eyes. He was wrong about so many things, her father. She hurried down the hall. As she closed the door to her room, she heard him say, 'I guess they had a tiff, huh?' and her mother hissed, 'Vernon!' but her voice was softened with amusement.

~

The next morning, a thin light appeared, enough to see the dense cloud cover, furrowed like soil after tilling. Ash fell gently. Everything was coated in dust.

The news the night before had shown the devastation – trees burnt and flattened, rivers flooded with melted snow, a landslide on the side of Mount Saint Helens the largest in known history. Several people were believed dead. A volcanologist, a photographer. The owner of a hunting lodge, a tough old man who'd vowed to stay despite the warnings. More bodies were expected to be found.

When Lori let the cat out, a grey haze blew in the door, sending Lori's mom rushing for the Hoover. Overnight, the silt had found its way through unseen gaps, onto kitchen lino and countertops, along shelves and inside cupboards. Health experts on the radio advised staying inside. But Lori wasn't afraid, not anymore. She watched the morning news to see the footage again – the tall grey plume rising like a miracle, miles above the earth.

Lori's father left to buy a few provisions. Her mother wandered about draping washing on chairs, the clothes soot-marked already. Angela sat writing a letter to their grandma in Spokane, her tongue between her teeth as she proclaimed in curling cursive, *We have even run out of cheese.* Lori pulled the cheddar from the back of the fridge and dumped it on the table, and Angela scowled.

Lori's bike was red topped with grey. She flicked the grime off her seat, and rode away. Her eyes watered, then cleared. The handkerchief she'd tied around her face made her breathing odd, somehow constricted, but she kept going. Apart from her breath and the swish of the bike, there was no other sound. She stopped at the corner and listened. The silence reminded her of winter, the smothering quiet of snow.

The main street was deserted apart from three cars near the food mart. She spotted her parents' station wagon and turned left, zigzagging through Harrington, passing the dead-end street where Travis lived before swinging back onto the highway north. There were houses dotted beside her, then a stretch of wheat for a mile or so. Everything was the colour of dirty silverware.

Just where the railway tracks hugged the highway on the right, Lori spotted the turn-off for Scott Road on the left. A few clapboard houses sat clumped together, not far from the junction. Lori rolled to a stop outside the closest one, where bands of pale-yellow paint showed below the grey. The roof was thick with ash. Dusty flowers flanked the front path in neat garden beds. A bike leant against the front steps, grey with a white underside.

Lori flicked out the kickstand, parked her bike beside the steps. Before she could approach, a woman with dark hair and eyes opened the door.

'Can I help you?' Her accent was like Joelle's, but stronger.

'Oh, hi.' Lori waved. 'I'm looking for Joelle. She's my friend.' Her cheeks blazed with heat beneath the handkerchief. 'I mean, she's in in my grade.'

The woman nodded. 'Alright then. Just a minute.' She disappeared, and Lori waited, shifting foot to foot. Time stretched, and she felt she'd been standing there for hours. All around her it was still, as if everything here was waiting too. She glanced back at the tracks her bike had made in the ash, thought about following them home.

'Hi, Lori.' Joelle stood in the doorway. She wore a halter-neck and shorts, her hair flowing to her waist. She stepped onto the narrow porch.

Lori inhaled through the cloth but she couldn't get air and she pulled the handkerchief down. Her lips were stiff with nerves. 'I didn't know where you lived. I decided to ask at each house.'

The new girl smiled, as if it all made perfect sense.

Lori smiled too. 'Want to come for a ride? I've been going crazy, cooped up inside.' She gestured to the stripy grey sky. 'Wild, right?'

'It really is.' Joelle looked back into the dark interior of the house, then met Lori's gaze. 'Give me a second?'

Lori forced herself to act cool. 'Sure.' Maybe they'd be friends. Maybe they'd be best friends. Her heart had swollen, expanding inside her like a giant red balloon.

When Joelle returned, she'd tied a rag across her face. Above the fabric, her eyes were a deep, steady brown. She rolled her bike from beside the steps.

'So,' she said. 'Where to now?'

ACKNOWLEDGEMENTS

This book would not exist without the kindness and guidance of others.

Many thanks to:

My publisher, Aviva Tuffield, who chose *If You're Happy* for the Glendower Award (along with other judges), and who skilfully steered the manuscript to publication. Her input and support have been invaluable, and I cannot thank her enough.

My editor, Felicity Dunning, who worked tirelessly to help make *If You're Happy* the book it has become. I'm so grateful for her meticulous attention to the manuscript.

The entire team at UQP for their assistance and expertise, and for publishing my very first book.

The State Library of Queensland, the Queensland Literary Awards, the judges of the Glendower Award and Jenny Summerson, for their commitment to the arts and for the Glendower Award, which has brought *If You're Happy* into the light.

Josh Durham, for his arresting and beguiling cover art.

Hannah Richell and the Hachette team, who selected an excerpt of this manuscript (in an earlier version) for the 2018 Richell Prize shortlist – a real honour.

The Katharine Susannah Prichard Foundation, who, in awarding me a 2017 KSP Fellowship, made me finally believe I might have something to say.

Publishers, judges and editors who selected stories for competitions, anthologies or literary magazines – in particular TJ Robinson, who published my very first story in *The Suburban Review*. Each time it's been an absolute thrill.

The writing community: a warm and welcoming group who cheer each other on, and whose Brisbane contingency is just magnificent.

The writing teachers who found something to admire in my early, clumsy work, and who fuelled the fire that kept me writing – especially writers Edwina Shaw and Angela Slatter.

Authors Nick Earls, Cate Kennedy and Mirandi Riwoe, for reading a draft version of the manuscript, and for their support. Thank you so much.

Poet and critic and lovely friend Felicity Plunkett, for sharing her wisdom; generous author and editor Susan Midalia, whose manuscript evaluation (her donation to the Authors for Fireys auction) gave me the confidence to enter the Glendower Award. Writers Louise Allan, Mandy Beaumont, Laura Elvery, Ashley Kalagian-Blunt, Cass Moriarty and Kali Napier, for various reasons including being wonderful.

My brilliant writing group, the Dead Darlings Society, who have been instrumental in any writing success: Deanna Antonelli, Mary Chang, Dan Fallon, Karen Hollands, Kaja Holzheimer, Nikki Mottram, Nicky Peelgrane, Fiona Reilly,

Paul Thomas and Warren Ward.

My close friends and fellow writers, Karen Hollands and Amanda O'Callaghan, for giving of their time and knowledge year after year, but above all for their friendship.

My work colleagues, including the Australian Surgical Assisting crew, and surgeon Scott Ingram and his team, who have followed the book's progress with much enthusiasm.

Friends from throughout my lifetime who have taken an interest, read stories and encouraged me – it means more than you could know. Special mentions to Carlie Faint, my beautiful friend of almost forty years, who never stopped telling me I could do this, and to my dear friend Craig Mackie, who helped convince me (with a very long email) to take the first step towards a writing career. Thank you also to treasured friends Heather Bulman and Kirsten Reid.

My mother and father, Leonie and Bruce – both retired teachers with the sharpest of minds – who love books and reading, and who are always on my side.

My siblings, Lachlan, Julene, Cameron and Kirk; my stepmum, Joy, my stepdad, John, and my extended family, for their genuine excitement about this book, which is everything anyone could hope for from their kin.

My children, Laura and Ben, who have been there through all the ups and downs, and who I adore.

Peter, my one and only, who knew I was afraid to chase this dream and who told me to go for it anyway.

~

Versions of the following stories have been previously published elsewhere:

'Tempest' in *TSS Publishing* (online), January 2021.
'All This Beauty' in the *Newcastle Short Story Award Anthology 2019*, Hunter Writers Centre, 2019.
'Descent' in *Pigface and Other Stories* (Margaret River Press), June 2018, and again in the *Aesthetica Creative Writing Annual*, 2019.
'A Shift in the Ice' in the *adda, online* magazine of Commonwealth Writers – the cultural initiative of the Commonwealth Foundation, July 2020.
'The Ground Beneath' in *Gargouille*, Issue 3 (2015), and also in the *Boroondara Literary Awards Anthology*, 2015.
'A Slow Exhalation' in the anthology *Thrill Me* (Glimmer Press), March 2020.
'Christmas Party' in *Kill Your Darlings*, February 2017.
'Boxing Day' in *Island Online*, 2021.

The title 'And You May Ask Yourself' is drawn from the Talking Heads song 'Once In A Lifetime'. Words and music by Brian Eno, David Byrne, Christopher Frantz, Jerry Harrison and Tina Weymouth. Copyright © 1980 by EG Music Ltd., WC Music Corp. and Index Music, Inc. All rights for EG Music Ltd. in the United States and Canada administered by Universal Music – MGB Songs. All rights for Index Music, Inc. administered by WC Music Corp. International copyright secured. All rights reserved. Reprinted by permission of Hal Leonard LLC.